Caleb and Mary Ruth have become teenagers, it is now the 70's, and they are doing more and more for the Lord. They now bring many young people to Jesus Christ. They received four very close friends that will help them teach their Christian believes. They are hoping to really help the world more and more, and bring more and more people to the Lord and Savior, Jesus Christ

This is the third book of the series, "The Chronicals of Caleb and Mary Ruth." They are now starting to meet their true destiny that they were born for.

Thank you for sharing book 3 of "The Chronicles of Caleb and Mary Ruth." They are really growing up now. It was neat to see them witnessing to their peers in school and the eventual salvation of Mike. Appreciated the love story of Sandy and Len and the way they faced life's challenges. Another cliff hanger! I know now we have to read book 4 to find out why Sandy doesn't want to have a baby yet.

Thank you for sharing your great work with us. It's apparent, through your writing, that you believe that we serve an all powerful God. Amen." Love and Blessings.

Pastor Tom and Julie

Very exciting! A lot of action with many surprises. A very good book!

Barb Smith

"The Chronicals of Caleb and Mary Ruth introduces vital spiritual concepts for young people. They weave practical spiritual knowledge into fascinating life events that hold the interest of the reader and provide valuable insights for living in todays culture.

Dr. Betty West

THE CHRONICLES OF CALEB AND MARY RUTH (SERIES)

CHILDREN OF DESTINY
(Book 1)

WE WILL NEVER GIVE UP
(Book 2)

Learn, Believe, and Obey

THE CHRONICLES OF CALEB AND MARY RUTH

Barbara L. Apicella

authorHOUSE®

AuthorHouse™
1663 Liberty Drive
Bloomington, IN 47403
www.authorhouse.com
Phone: 1-800-839-8640

First published by AuthorHouse 3/30/2011

ISBN: 978-1-4567-5110-4 (e)
ISBN: 978-1-4567-5111-1 (dj)
ISBN: 978-1-4567-5112-8 (sc)

Library of Congress Control Number: 2011903944

Printed in the United States of America

Acknowledgment

Again my thanks is to my Lord and Savior, Jesus Christ, for all He has done for me throughout my entire life. He, and His Father, God, are still leading me to write these books. The things that are said in my books about the Lord are true and will help you become reborn in Him. I pray that more and more people will become good Christian believers and also to learn, believe, and obey the Bible.

Chapter 1

Pieces of the ceiling and the roof started falling down. Most of the people were running out the doors. Len dived over Caleb and Mary Ruth to protect them. Tom jumped off the stage and landed on Thelma. Suddenly, the whole roof started falling down! Most of the audience had already made it outside. Luckily, the theater had many doors that were able to be used.

The police, fire trucks, and ambulances, were on the way. When they arrived, they couldn't believe their eyes! The whole theater had collapsed. There were many people outside, most of the ones that ran out of the theater, but many more were coming to see what happened.

All the firemen and the police were trying to move things so they could check to see if there were any survivors inside. There wasn't very much light out side but luckily they did have flashlights. They had to be very careful when they moved things so it wouldn't cause more things to fall. They hadn't checked much when they found an unconscious woman under some debree. She was still alive and the ambulance took her straight to the hospital.

They came across several more men and women who had broken bones and a few other things wrong with them, but nothing really bad. They all were taken to the hospital.

Captain Hardy arrived. He didn't go to the show because he didn't feel good. He watched it on TV at his home. Suddenly the show just went off. At first he thought it was his TV, but then he realized that something must have happened at the theater.

When he got there he was shocked to see what happened. He did hear the unbelievable thunder that was so very loud, but never thought anything bad happened.

"How are things going?" he asked one of his officers. The officer updated him on all they found so far.

"What about Caleb, Mary Ruth, Len and all the others that were in the show?"

"So far we haven't found any of them yet. They were in the middle of the theater and up on the stage, so we have to keep moving a lot of things to get to them."

Captain Hardy started helping them. They finally came to a large section of the roof that was not broken. It was a huge piece that fell down at once. They moved it as much as they could and crawled into a small area where the first row of the seats were located. The big piece of the roof was completely leaning on the stage.

As they entered, they could hear people crying. Captain Hardy yelled, "We're on our way to help you all."

A woman's voice yelled back, "Please hurry and get us out of here before more things cave in on us!"

They found Jane and Josh on the floor; apparently they jumped off their seat and laid on the floor. Very good choice!

On the other side of them, they could see Tom and it seemed like someone was under him. They cleared a lot of the things out very carefully and pulled the four of them out. Luckily, they were all in pretty good shape. They found that it was Thelma who was under Tom.

They all were taken to the hospital to be checked out. Captain Hardy said, "Now we have to somehow get on the stage. Let us pray that we can do it and everyone is alive." They all folded their hands and prayed their own prayers to God and asked Him to please help them.

About forty five minutes later, they were able to move a large part of the ceiling and the roof. When they did, they saw everyone.

They all looked unconscious, hopefully. They were able to reach Sandy first. They pulled her out. She was alive, but remained unconscious.

Next was Len and they saw that he was laying over Caleb and Mary Ruth. The kids were now conscious. They said that they were fine, as tears flowed down their face. Caleb cried, "Len kept us from getting hurt."

Mary Ruth said, "We know that something very heavy hit him and also Tim who was sitting next to us.

The kids were rushed to the hospital with Len and Sandy.

Next was Tim, then Paul and Al. They were also rushed to the hospital.

The police officers and firemen stayed there many more hours, to make sure there were no other people under the debree.

As they were searching, Captain Hardy asked, "What in the world made something like this happen? I know there was a tremendous amount of very loud thunder. I really heard it, and I guess there was a lot of lighting. It's even hard to believe lighting could have caused this. There had to be a tornado go by, but of all places, why did it only hit the theater?"

As Caleb and Mary Ruth had gone to the hospital with Len and Sandy, tears were running down their face. Suddenly, Len's heart stopped beating. The two paramedics gave him CPR. Mary Ruth and Caleb touched Len and prayed to God that his heart would start again. After several minutes his heart did start beating again. Caleb and Mary Ruth hugged each other and thanked God.

When they got to the ER, a doctor immediately checked Len and sent him for x-rays, then to ICU. They checked Tim next and did mainly the same thing. They were both in the worse shape compared to everyone else. Most of the patients had a few broken bones, some were in good shape, but Len and Tim were the worse.

Sandy had already been checked in the ambulance, she was awake when she reached the hospital and they checked her again, she had no problem and they told her to go out in the waiting room. She saw them wheel Len past her and could see that he was still unconscious. She ran up to the desk and asked where they were taking him.

The lady replied, "I don't know, but I'll try to find out for you." Sandy told her that she is Len's fiancée.

The lady went inside and asked if anyone knew how Len was doing, as his fiancée is out in the waiting room.

The doctor who examined Len said, "I'll talk to her for a minute and tell her what's going on."

He went out to the waiting room and asked for Len's fiancée, as it was full of people. Sandy jumped up and ran over to him. .

The doctor said, "Len is headed to the x-ray department and after that he'll be going straight to ICU. I believe his neck is broken."

Sandy nearly fainted! "Oh no!"

"I'm sorry, but I have to go back and check more people."

"My mom and dad, the kids, and a lot of other people are still in there."

"We will be checking them all and either keep them here or send them home, depending on their condition." He then walked back to be with more patients.

Sandy sat down and cried. The next one to come out was Thelma, her left arm was in a sling. Her and Sandy hugged each other and sat down.

Sandy told her about Len's condition. Thelma held her hand and said, "I can't believe this happened!" As she said that, Jane and Josh appeared. They were both basically fine. They all hugged and kissed each other. Sandy decided to wait to tell them about Len.

Josh said, "I wonder how Tom is doing? Thelma, he jumped on top of you to protect you."

"He did? I thought he just fell on me. I hope he's okay!"

About ten minutes later Tom did appear on a pair of crutches. His right leg had a brace on it. They all hugged and sat down and waited for the rest of them. Luckily, they were told that just about all of the audience was ok. Only a few were hurt. The worse part of the cave in was on the stage.

Al appeared with a bandage on his head, and was in pretty good shape. About fifteen minutes later, Paul came out with just some black and blue marks and some cuts.

Thelma said, "All we need now is Caleb and Mary Ruth."

Jane asked, What about Len and Tim? Where are they? Did they leave already?"

More tears ran down Sandy's face. "I do know that Tim was really hurt and went to ICU." As she was about to talk about Len, Caleb and Mary Ruth came out and hugged everyone. They were also doing okay.

Caleb asked, "Where is Len? Is he okay?"

"We rode in the ambulance with him. You were there too, Sandy, but you were unconscious. His heart stopped beating, but they brought him back," Mary Ruth cried.

"He saved our life," cried Caleb. Tears were running from their eyes.

Sandy looked at everyone and started crying more. "He's in ICU. They think that Len has a broken neck. I only saw him for a second as they were taking him to the x-ray department."

Everyone started crying. They all held hands and thanked the Lord that so many people were okay, and prayed for Len and Tim's recovery.

Jane said, "Why don't you all go back to the house and I'll stay here with Sandy.

Caleb asked, "Can Mary Ruth and I please stay?"

"Of course," said Sandy.

Paul said, "I'll find someone to give me a ride down to where the cars were parked and I'll come and pick you all up. Just take it easy."

As Paul was walking out the door, Captain Hardy was coming in. They hugged each other. Paul told him how everyone was. Captain Hardy was so sad to hear about Len's condition and that Tim was also in bad shape. "Thank God no one else is in a very bad condition."

Paul told the captain where he was going and Captain Hardy replied, "Hop in my car and I'll take you down to get yours. Then I'm going to come back here and try to find out more about Len's condition."

Paul got Sandy's car and came back to the hospital and picked up Josh, Thelma, Tom, and Al and took them all back to the Phillip's house. After they got there, Paul made them all a little something to eat, then went back to the hospital.

Thelma, Tom and Al, were sitting in the living room with Josh. Josh put the TV on. It was showing what happened to the St. Cloud movie theater and talking about how everyone was doing. There were many people in the area that had been in the audience. A lot of them were being interviewed and telling their story about what happened.

One man said, "We were all watching everyone on stage tell what they had been through. It was so interesting. Then, suddenly, we heard the loudest noises we had never heard in our lives. It kept getting louder and louder. It sounded like thunder. It was totally unbelievable! The electricity went off and parts of the ceiling started falling down. I even thought I heard a loud voice say something strange, but I'm sure it was just someone screaming. Everyone started running out the doors and luckily most of us made it out before the roof caved in. What an experience! We know that the biggest part of the roof collapsed on the stage. We don't know yet how those people are doing but we will definitely pray for them."

"Thank you." This is Sue Brown reporting for ABC." It then went back to the main news program.

The main man, Lurk Burk said, "One of out ABC reporters, Tim Smith, was on that stage. As we get any information on how they're all doing, we will let you know."

Sandy, Jane and the kids were sitting in the waiting room outside of ICU. They weren't saying anything, but they all were praying in their mind.

A few minutes later, a doctor came out and sat down beside them. He didn't smile. He said, "We x-rayed Len all over, since he is unconscious. We found several things that are broken. Three vertebrae in his neck and two in his lower spine. Truthfully, I have to tell you that things don't look very good for him. He's still unconscious and lying flat. He can't be moved for any reason. I think that he may be paralyzed from the neck down, but we won't know for sure until he becomes conscious. You can go up and see him, but just for a few minutes."

They were all crying when they heard that news. Jane asked, "What about Tim Smith? How is he doing?"

"He is conscious, but not really with it. He has two broken legs, a broken right hip and a partially fractured skull. I'm pretty sure that he'll recover completely, but it will take quite awhile."

"At least there is hope for him. Our hope is that the Lord will heal Len."

"That is truly my hope too," replied the doctor.

Sandy, Jane, Caleb, and Mary Ruth entered Len's unit. He was lying so peacefully and quiet. They all touched him and prayed for him. They all kissed his cheek and told him that they loved him and always will.

When they left Len's unit, they went over to see Tim Smith. He was awake. They all smiled at him and Jane told him that the doctor told them that eventually he would be well again. Tears ran down his cheeks.

He mumbled, "I am so sorry, this is my entire fault! I'm the one that decided to have the TV event at the theater."

Sandy said, "Please don't blame yourself, you, in no way, knew that there would be a storm tonight. You were trying to make it a great show."

"Don't ever blame yourself, no one else is blaming you either," Caleb said.

Tim smiled and said, "Thank you for saying that."

Sandy didn't tell him that it probably was Satan again, trying to get rid of Caleb and Mary Ruth. She also heard tremendously loud words, "Goodbye Forever," but didn't mention it to anyone."

After they prayed for him, they stopped at the nurses desk and gave them their phone number. Jane said, "Please call us if anything happens to Len."

The nurse replied, "Don't worry, we'll call you right away."

They then found out who all were put in the hospital from the theater and went to see them all. Luckily, they all were in pretty good shape. Jane said, "Of all the people that were hurt, Len is surly the worse, I pray he lives."

"He's only hurt the worse because he saved us," cried Mary Ruth. Tears were running down Caleb's face also.

Sandy hugged them both and said, "Kids don't feel bad. Len wanted to save you both. He loves you both and knows you have a great destiny in your future, we all want you to live. If he hadn't jumped on you kids, you probably would have been killed."

Caleb said, "Len is such a wonderful person for saving Mary Ruth's and my life. We will pray for him and do everything that we can do so he can live."

"Truly we will!" cried Mary Ruth.

Chapter 2

Jane called her husband, Josh. He and Paul drove down town and picked up his car, drove over to the hospital, picked them up and went home.

Josh said, "Believe it or not, there still is a bunch of people around the theater, plus police and firemen still checking things out. That was the weirdest thing that ever happened! I could hardly believe that something like that could ever occur. Thank God that no one was killed! How is Len doing?"

"Let's wait till we get home, so I can tell everyone," stated Sandy.

When they arrived home, Jane and Sandy told them about Len and the bad condition he's in. Tim was also in ICU, but will probably recover, and about everyone else that they visited in the hospital. They all were so sad, they got down on their knees, held hands and prayed for everyone and thanked the Lord that so many people weren't hurt at all.

"How about we all make our own sandwiches when we get hungry? I'll put all the things out on the kitchen table and you can help yourselves, okay?" asked Jane. They all said "Okay."

Sandy walked out the back door and sat on the swing and cried. Paul saw where she went and followed her. He sat down beside her and put his arm around her.

"Sandy, we all love Len, we also know how you both were planning your wedding. You must think positive, negative thoughts aren't good. They stress you out and you can become ill. At least he is alive and he saved Caleb and Mary Ruth. I'm sure he will be getting the best treatment there is. He's being watched and taken care of around the clock. We will all continually pray to God that he lives, but we don't know how long it will take him to recover. Have patience, Sandy."

She laid her head on Paul's shoulder and said, "Thank you so much, you're right. We must think positively, not negatively and we must have faith."

Paul said, "Let's pray." They both said a loving prayer to the Lord, and then went back inside.

"Sandy, what kind of sandwich would you like? I want to make it for you."

Sandy replied, "Just some butter on the bread, ham, cheese, tomato, and mayonaise. That would be great."

Paul made the same sandwich for both of them and they sat down and ate.

"Thank you so much, Paul, that was really sweet of you and the sandwich is delicious." As they were finishing, it seemed like everyone else came in and started making their sandwiches.

Sandy said, "Let's get out of their way." They went in the living room and watched TV. A little while later, everybody joined them.

As they were watching a show, it was interrupted by the news station. The station told everyone that they just wanted to inform them that there were no other people lying under the roof at the theater. "That is great news! See you again at 11 PM." The show came back on.

Mary Ruth said, "Again, thank the Lord that no one else was hurt!"

"Yes, that is really wonderful!" replied Caleb.

The 11PM news told the whole story again. They talked about their reporter, Tim Smith's condition, and also Len's, and how he saved Caleb and Mary Ruth from being killed.

Thelma said, "Come on kids, let's go to bed. You don't have to go to school tomorrow. We can all just take it easy, pray for everyone, and thank God for helping us."

"We all would like to go and see the people in the hospital, especially Len," Tom said.

Sandy replied, "We can all go and see Len, but remember, he is unconscious, but maybe he'll be awake tomorrow. I sure hope so."

Al said, "We all hope so."

They all said goodnight and went to bed. Thelma was so tired, the minute she laid down she fell sound asleep.

Caleb and Mary Ruth started talking to each other. Caleb said, "We have to pray constantly all day long for Len, whenever we can. We might have to pray for a long time because it is up to the Lord when he will be healed or if he will be healed."

"I agree and the Lord will understand that we keep praying because we love Len and want him to be healed, not because we don't think that we keep praying because he didn't listen to us."

"Your right, Mary Ruth, he does know how much we love Len and are so grateful to him for saving our lives. Tomorrow, when we go to see him, we will hold his hand and pray."

"We must have total faith and trust in the Lord always," replied Mary Ruth.

They both prayed for Len and everyone else who was hurt. They then got in bed and fell asleep.

The next morning they all got up around the same time, ate breakfast, then drove to the hospital. They all visited everyone from the theater and prayed for them. Len was still unconscious, but Tim Smith was feeling a little bit better. By noon, they all went back to the house and had lunch.

Sandy went back to the hospital to be with Len. Paul went down to the police station to talk to Captain Hardy. They all kept praying for Len's recovery.

The next day, Jane and Thelma drove Caleb and Mary Ruth to school. Everyone at school was so happy to see them, but only two of the boys who were so mean to Caleb. Caleb started to get a little friendly with them. He knew that he had to teach them about Jesus and have them change their attitudes.

Four days later, Len finally became conscious. Sandy was sitting with him when he opened his eyes. She jumped up and held his hand. Len looked all around and said, "Where am I?"

Sandy told him about everything that happened.

"I kind of remember the loud noises that we were hearing and jumping on top of Caleb and Mary Ruth, but I don't remember anything after that."

"Len, you've been unconscious for five days. We all prayed that you would live and our prayers were answered."

Len wanted to roll over and hug and kiss Sandy. "Sandy, what's wrong with me? I can't move!"

"Len, relax. You have broken vertebrae in your neck and lower spine.

I don't know how long it will take you to recover. You must have patience and faith in God."

"I am so shocked! You mean I was unconscious for five days?"

"The doctors and nurses care for you and you have an IV, but now that you are conscious, I'm sure you can be fed."

"What time is it?"

"It's 2:15 PM in the afternoon."

"Why aren't you at work?"

"I don't care about my job, I care about you."

Len looked at her and said, "Sandy, I might never recover, or if I do, it might take quite a long time. I want you to go to your job. You can always visit me after work or on weekends."

"Do you know that many people come to see you everyday, but I want to be with you all day and everyday? I love you so and I always will, no matter if you recover or not!"

"I love you to Sandy, but I don't want to run your life."

"Len, I'll take care of you forever, I want to. Let me tell you about all of our friends. My mom and dad are doing fine; they're at home right now. Thelma is fine, apparently, when things stated falling, Tom jumped on her so she wouldn't be hurt to badly. Tom has a broken right leg. Al is fine, he just had his head hit, but it wasn't bad. Right now he's up at his house in Orlando, but he calls every day to check on you. I forgot to tell you, Tom is going back to his home in PA tomorrow, also, Thelma is having someone bring all her household things down here to put in storage until Joel and Connie leave the home she is buying. She and the kids will then move in. Her house in PA might also be sold soon. Someone did make a down payment on it. Paul is going to the police office course and he is doing fine. The kids are back at school again. They will all be here later to see you. They come everyday and hold your hands and pray for you. By the way, Tim Smith is now in a regular hospital room. He can't do much with all his broken bones, but he is doing much better. Everyone else who was hurt has gone home and is doing okay."

"I think that I should go out and let the nurses know that you are awake! They can call your doctor to come and see you. I'll be right back!"

Sandy ran out to the nurse's desk and said, "Guess what? Len is awake! We've already talked for awhile."

The two nurses jumped up and hugged Sandy. "Thank God! We're going in to see him!"

When they went in the room, they smiled at Len and held his hand, which he couldn't even feel.

The nurse, Diane, said, "We're so thankful to the Lord that you became conscious! We're going to call Dr. Blankenship right away and let him know the good news."

They went back to the desk and called the doctor. He said, "What wonderful news! I'll be there in just a few minutes."

About ten minutes later, Dr. Blankenship arrived. He said, "Congratulations Len! All we have to do now is get you moving again and we will do everything we can to do that. I'll put you on a liquid diet for now. One of the nurses will feed you and we'll see how you do. If you do fine on the liquids, we'll then put you on a soft diet. I am so happy for you! Also, after you take enough liquids we can discontinue the IV."

After the doctor left, Sandy went out to the desk and called home and told them the wonderful news. They all praised God!

Thelma said, "I can't wait to tell Caleb and Mary Ruth the wonderful news."

"Josh and Tom can go over and see Len now, and when we pick the kids up after school, we'll go right over," said Jane.

"Thank you so much, Jane. That is so nice of you!" Thelma replied.

Josh and Tom were about to leave, Josh said, "Make sure you let Al know the good news and call Captain Hardy and tell him to make sure he tells Paul."

When Josh and Tom arrived at ICU, they went in to see Len. They both kissed him on the cheek and told him how very happy they were.

Tom said, "I'm leaving tomorrow to go back to PA. and I'm so glad that you became conscious before I left. I will keep praying for your complete recovery. I will also have Pastor Kramer, Pastor Holman, and their congregations pray for you and anyone else I can tell!"

Len smiled and said, "Thank you so much. I really appreciate it."

"You are a wonderful person, you saved Caleb and Mary Ruth. They love you so much! We all do!" replied Josh.

They stayed for a few more minutes, and then had to leave. The doctor was letting Sandy stay as long as she wanted to.

As they were leaving, the doctor was entering. He went in and smiled at Len. Len smiled back. Dr. Blankenship said, "Len, I'm going to do some things to you and I need you to let me know if you feel anything."

He started off squeezing Len's feet, ankles, knees, arms, hands, ect. Unfortunately Len felt nothing.

Len was very upset. The doctor said, "We have to perform more tests on you. Hopefully, after your vertebras heal, you will be able to move. We might have to do several operations. Just have confidence in us. We will do our best."

"Thank you," Len said.

"By the way doctor, we don't even remember your name," said Sandy.

He said, "Oh, I'm sorry, my name is Jeffery Blankenship."

Sandy shook his hand and said, ""Glad to meet you."

Jane called Al and gave him the good news. Al said, "Thank the Lord! I will be down tomorrow morning to see him. Thank you so much for letting me know!"

Jane then called Captain Hardy. He was so happy and said, "I will let Paul know right away. Everyone here will be so glad to hear this great news!"

Josh and Tom arrived home a little while later while Jane and Thelma went and picked the kids up.

Chapter 3

Caleb and Mary Ruth were surprised that the three boys weren't bothering them. Thank Heaven! They got in the car and Thelma told them the great news.

"How wonderful!" Mary Ruth cried.

Caleb cried, "We can't wait to see him!"

"We're on our way to the hospital right now," Jane said. The kids clapped their hands and hugged each other.

When they got to ICU, Jane and Thelma let the kids go to see Len first. They ran in, hugged and kissed him. Len smiled at them and said, "Hi, my two favorite kids. I'm so glad to see you both again."

Mary Ruth said, "We thank you so much for saving our lives."

"We are so very sorry that you have been hurt so badly. Please forgive us!" cried Caleb.

Len said, "Listen kids, I love you both and I truly wanted to save your lives, no matter what happened to me. Please don't feel bad, I'm alive and I'll love you both forever."

"We love you so much also," cried Mary Ruth.

"We will always pray for your complete recovery. I don't know how long it will take, but we all must have complete faith in the Lord," replied Caleb.

"Okay kids," said Sandy. "Lets let Jane and Thelma come on in to see Len."

The kids hugged and kissed Len goodbye. May Ruth said, "We'll see you tomorrow." They went out and sat down, then Jane and Thelma went in.

"Oh Len," Thelma said, "We are so happy and grateful to the Lord! It's so nice to be able to talk to you again."

Jane hugged him and said, "I love you! I called Al and he will be down to see you tomorrow and I also called Captain Hardy and I'm sure Paul will see you when he gets out of his class. Everyone is so happy for you." They talked for a few more minutes until their time was up.

Sandy said to Len, "I'll be right back. I'll walk them out to the car." When they got out in the waiting room, tears started flowing down Sandy's face. "Sandy, what's wrong?" asked her mom.

"I am so thankful that Len became conscious, but Dr. Blankenship came and checked his whole body. Len could not feel anything."

Jane said, "I'm sure it's going to take awhile until his recovers."

"Don't be sad, you know to think positive and have faith. It will happen when it is the right time," said Caleb.

Mary Ruth replied, "We will help you take care of him. We'll do anything for him!"

Sandy hugged them and said, "Thank you kids. I love you and I am glad that Len saved your life. I know we must have faith and be patient." They all got in the car and left. Sandy went back up to be with Len.

Captain Hardy went and told Paul the good news about Len. Paul said, "Thank You Dear God!" They hugged each other.

"I'm going to go and see him as soon as I leave here."

Captain Hardy asked, "Do you mind if I come with you?"

"Of course not! Len will be glad to see you!"

After Paul's class was finished, they went over to the hospital. They went up to ICU and went in to see Len. They tried to shake his hand and became aware that he could not move it. They talked to him and told him how thankful they were that he was conscious. Sandy was out at that time getting something to eat.

They left when their ten minutes was up. As they walked back to their cars, they talked about how Len was not able to move his hands. Paul said, "We must keep on praying until he is healed."

"I certainly will," stated Captain Hardy. "He's one of the best police officers I ever had work for me. I want him back!"

Paul took Captain Hardy back to the police station. They said, "Goodbye, see you tomorrow," then Paul left.

Sandy returned to Len's unit and Len said, "You just missed Paul and Captain Hardy. They came to see me." Len smiled at Sandy and said, "Sandy, it might take me a very long time to recover. I want you to go back to your new job. I thank you so much that you want to stay with me. Maybe you can start saving money for our wedding."

"But Len, I love you and want to help you!"

"I know you love me, you can come and see me every night after work and on weekends. Please do what I'm asking! I'm very sleepy right now. Go home and eat with your parents, the kids, and our friends. Call Captain Hardy tomorrow and tell him you will return."

Sandy felt very said, but she said, "Okay, if that's what you want me to do, I'll do it. Just remember that I love you and always will." She kissed Len and said, "See you tomorrow."

When she left, the nurse, Diane, entered the room. "Are you ready for your liquid dinner?"

Len said, "Sure, I can't wait!"

After she fed him, he looked at her very sadly and said, "I am in tremendous pain, can you give me something for it?"

"Of course I can. I'll be right back."

Len still had his IV so she gave it to him through that so it would work faster.

"How long do you think it will take me to recover?"

"You will have to ask Dr. Blankenship about that." She had no idea how long it would take him to recover, of if he ever would.

The next day, Sandy called Captain Hardy and told him what Len said. She said, "If you want me, I'll be glad to come back."

"Don't be surprised, but I was holding the job for you, hoping that you would come back. I know you will do great. You can start again tomorrow morning."

"Thank you so much!" Sandy replied.

Jane, Josh and Thelma dropped the kids off at school, and then took Tom to the airport for his return to PA. They stayed with him until the plane was ready to leave.

Tom hugged Jane and Josh and thanked them for everything. He then went up to Thelma, hugged her, and gave her a big kiss. "I wish we would have met in PA. Thelma, your such a nice person."

"I will be coming up to PA. pretty soon. I have to hire someone to pack up the things in my house so I can bring them back to Florida. I'll soon be moving into a beautiful house here."

"Well, let me know when you're coming and I will be glad to help you, no charge!"

"That will be great!" Thelma said. "I'll let you know when I'm coming. Have a great trip!"

"Thanks Thelma, hope to see you soon! Bye!" Tom left and went to the plane.

The kids were eating lunch at school. Two of the boys, Jake and Henry sat down at their table. Caleb and Mary Ruth smiled and said, "Hello." The boys smiled back at them.

Jake said, "I guess your wondering what we're going to say to you. Don't worry, it won't be anything bad."

"We want to be friends with you. We realize that you both are really good people. We heard a lot about you this past week," said Henry.

"We'll be glad to be your friends," said Caleb. You can even go to church and Sunday school with us."

"We will be glad to do that. We never went to Sunday school before."

Mary Ruth smiled and said, "Sunday school will help you learn about Jesus, we will also help you. Where is Mike?"

"We told him what we were going to do today and he got mad at us. He still thinks that he's the king of the school. Now, since he's alone, I hope the kids don't listen to his commands."

Caleb said, "I know we can tell the kids to depend on us to help them and not to do wrong."

"Amen!" said Mary Ruth. They all shook hands and went back to class.

Chapter 4

Sandy spent the whole day with Len. She told him that Tom was leaving to go back to PA. today, but he said he would keep in touch. Mom, dad and Thelma took him to the airport. I did call Captain Hardy this morning and told him that I wanted to return to work. Can you believe he was holding the job for me? That was so kind of him. So this is the last weekday that I'll be spending the whole day with you."

Len said, "That's okay, I will miss you but the nurses will take good care of me."

"I will come here everyday after work and of course, on the weekends."

After they picked the kids up at school, Jane, Josh, Thelma and the kids all went to visit Len.

Paul came over as soon as he finished his training. He told Len that he had only one more week to go until he was done, then he would start his job. He said, "Sandy, as soon as I save some money, I'll find my own place to stay."

Len replied, "Once you start your job, I'm sure you will be on day shift for awhile. You and Sandy can ride to work together."

"That would be great! A police officer picks me up every morning and brings me home after my training, since I don't have a car. I have to buy one someday."

When they all got home, they had supper, then watched the news. The phone rang. Jane answered it. The man asked for Thelma.

Thelma got on the phone and said, "Hello."

"This is Bob Petusky. Guess what! A young couple put a down payment on your house! We're having a mortgage company check if they are able to get a mortgage. If everything works out, your home will be sold within a month and a half."

"That's truly wonderful! I hope it happens! The people that I'm buying the home from down here will be leaving within a month. Maybe I won't have to put all my things in a storage unit. If it works out, I can put everything right in my new house!"

"I'll let you know what's happening. I think everything will work out."

"Thank you so much, Bob! Bye, bye."

Thelma hung the phone up and told everyone the good news. I have a lot of things to bring down, I do have a nice car that I can use, but I also have a beautiful pickup truck that was Joe's. I'm sure I'll never use it. Maybe I should ask Bob to put it up for sale."

Sandy said, "I have a good idea! Paul does not have anything to drive and he'll be done his training in a week. Then he will start getting paid. I bet he would like to buy it. Maybe he'll buy it from you!"

"I would love a pickup truck! Can you tell me something about it?" Paul asked.

"Well, it's a Ford and its red. The year is 1965. Joe had bought it before all these things happened. So now it's only about a year and a half old. I believe it has about three thousand miles on it."

"Boy, it really sounds great! How much do you want for it?"

"I don't really know at this point. I know we don't owe anything on it. When Joe bought it, he traded in his old truck and paid the rest in cash. Let me think about it and I'll let you know. I won't have it for at least a month anyway, so you can save some of your money."

Paul said, "How lucky can I be?"

Jane announced, ""Let's not forget that two weeks from this Thursday is Thanksgiving. Then before you know it, Christmas will be here!"

Days passed. Sandy was doing well at her job. She visited Len everyday. The doctor decided to put him in a regular room as he was doing well except he couldn't move from his neck down. He had to be cared for constantly.

Everyone still visited him and prayed for his recovery. A few days later, the doctor decided to send him to a nursing home where he could be taken care of. He had no need to be in the hospital. They all visited him there everyday.

Dr. Blankenship told Sandy that he was trying to get in touch with a very famous orthopedic doctor in New York. This doctor did amazing recoveries for patients like Len. His name was Dr. Jerald Yost.

Sandy said, "Please, that would be so wonderful if he could help Len."

"Believe me, I'll never stop trying to contact him. He is always so busy. He even goes to other countries to help people."

The kids were doing fine at school and now had many friends, although Mike wouldn't come near them.

Thanksgiving came and they all had a wonderful dinner, then they all took the food down to Len at the nursing home. Sandy fed him as much as he could eat. He was put on a wheel chair so now he did look better because he was sitting up.

Paul was finished with his training and was now working at the police station. Al came down at least twice a week and visited Len. Tom always called to see how he was doing. The kids prayed and prayed for Len's recovery, as did everyone else.

A week later, Thelma got a call from Bob Petusky. He said, "Great news! The couple will be able to buy your house for the amount you were asking. It should be completed about January 3rd."

Thelma was so happy; she knew Connie and Joel were moving around December 15th, which means the house will be empty at that time. She can now fly up to PA and get all her things loaded in a truck and bring them down to St. Cloud, then put them right in her new home. She contacted Connie and told her about her house being sold. Now she will completely pay them around the 5th of January. They were so happy that everything worked out so well. Now they can start looking for a house as soon as they arrive in Ohio.

Everyone was so happy for Thelma. The kids were excited to live with her and still be close to the Phillips. Thelma made a flight reservation for December 14th. She called Tom and told him the good news.

"What airport are you flying to?" Tom asked.

"I'll be flying to Philadelphia on December 14th. I'll be landing there around 2pm."

"I'll be glad to pick you up and take you to your home. I'd like to see it anyway since I'll be helping you pack the truck."

"That would really be great! I was just going to call one of my friends and ask them to come and pick me up."

"I'll be more than glad to! By the way, I visited Pastor Holman and Pastor Kramer. We had lunch together and I told them the whole story of what happened and thanked them for their prayers. Tell Sandy and Len that they and their congregations will continue to pray for Len's recovery, no matter how long it takes."

"That is wonderful! I feel so very sorry for Len's condition. This was the second time he saved my grandchildren, with the Lord's help. He is a wonderful man and I will always help him in any way I can. I'll be calling you soon, Tom. Bye!"

On December 13th, Thelma called Tom back and reminded him that she would be at the Philadelphia airport tomorrow at 2 pm.

"I'm all ready to come and pick you up. In fact, I already rented a large truck for you, and several of my friends will help us load it. We just have to let them know when and they'll be there."

"Thank you so much! Before I leave PA, I'm going to see all my friends and tell them goodbye and invite them to come down and visit me. I also will be seeing Pastor Holman, who was with me and helped me so much, also Pastor Kramer. I really don't know where Pastor Holman and Pastor Kramer live."

"I just visited them recently, if you want, I'll be glad to take you to see them. In fact, I will buy you all lunch."

"That will be great! See you tomorrow!"

Everyone was getting ready for Christmas. Now Caleb and Mary Ruth had their lunch at a large table and many kids who became their friends sat with them.

One day while they were eating lunch, Mary Ruth said, "One of the best days ever will soon be here."

A girl, named Cindy said, "You mean Christmas."

"Of course!" replied Mary Ruth.

"Yes, Santa Claus will be coming and bringing us lots of gifts," Cindy replied.

"Yes, it's nice to get gifts but the best thing is that we use this as the day Jesus was born," stated Mary Ruth.

One of the other girls said, "I heard that, but who is Jesus?"

A girl was sitting aside of Mary Ruth named Tammy, and she was becoming her best friend. She said, "You mean you don't know who Jesus is? Jesus Christ is our Lord and Savior. He died on the cross so our sins would be forgiven. He is the Son of God. He is our everything!"

Mary Ruth hugged Tammy and said, "I'm glad you know about our Lord and what He did for us. The Lord has saved Caleb and me so many times. If any of you would like to join us on Sundays at our Sunday school class, we would be glad to have you come with us. Just let us know."

"Our father was a pastor and we have learned a lot about the Bible. We keep reading and learning more and more. We understand more as time goes by. I'm hoping that someday, Mary Ruth and I can teach others about the old and new testaments in the Bible," stated Caleb. He also thought to himself, I love how Tammy knows about Jesus.

Cindy said, "I would love to learn more about Jesus and the Bible." All the others smiled and said, "Me too!"

They all went back to their class rooms after lunch. Mary Ruth and Tammy were in the same room.

"Tammy, I'm so glad that you know about Jesus," said Mary Ruth.

"My grandfather is a pastor at Christ Lutheran Church in Kissimmee, which is only about ten miles from here. I get to see him a lot, in fact, we go to church there. I guess I already know a pretty lot about Jesus. I read the Bible everyday and of course I pray."

"That's really wonderful," Mary Ruth replied. "You could probably be with Caleb and me to help others learn about Jesus. I do know that we also have a lot more to learn, when we get older we can really teach a lot more."

"That will be something that my heart would love to do!" said Tammy.

Dr. Yost, the famous doctor from New York, got in touch with Dr. Blankenship and told him he would come down and examine Len. He came down a few days before Christmas and checked Len. He told Dr. Blankenship that there was nothing he could do for Len at this time, but he would keep Len's name in his file and if something new is found to recover Len, he would come down to help him.

Dr. Blankenship told Len the circumstances and how Dr. Yost would keep him in his file.

Len was so disappointed he cried. He said to himself, "I will continue to have complete faith in the Lord and I know someday He will help me!"

Thelma had gone to PA. and met Tom at the airport. When she arrived at her home, she visited her friends and the Pastors and thanked them all for their love and prayers. Tom told Thelma that he would be glad to drive the truck to Florida. They would attach her pickup truck to a tow bar behind the big truck.. They put everything she wanted in the truck and left for Florida. Thelma drove her car. They stopped for two nights, and finally made it to St. Cloud.

Within the next week, they had everything moved into her new home. Tom stayed over Christmas and had a great time with everyone. Al came down and of course, Len, in his wheelchair was there. Tom and Thelma seemed to be getting very close to each other.

Len's condition was still the same. He hadn't got any better, but he hadn't got worse. He was so glad that he got to spend Christmas with everyone at Jane and Josh's home. They had a wonderful time, but inwardly Len was sad because of his condition. He wondered if he and Sandy would ever be married. What kind of life would we have if my condition stays like this? Sandy would mention the wedding plans but Len did not want to marry her while he was like this.

After the New Year, the kids went back to school and Tom helped Thelma move all of the kid's things to her new home. The kids each had their own bedroom. Thelma had the master bedroom and they even had a spare bedroom.

As they were moving the things over, Tom said to Thelma, "I have to fly back to PA. in a couple of days."

"If you would like to still stay in my spare bedroom until you leave, you're welcomed to."

"That would be nice to be down here by the lake and of course to be with you and the kids. Thanks, I will."

Paul was now driving himself to work in his beautiful red pick up truck. He was so happy to see it when Tom and Thelma arrived! She gave him a great price and he could pay her monthly until it was paid off. Now he has to save money to put a down payment on a small house. Since the kids moved out, he's staying in that room and Sandy is back in her room.

The kids were doing well at school. They formed a Bible study for their friends, every Wednesday night on their back porch. They all attended the Sunday school classes every Sunday.

Mary Ruth and Tammy grew closer and closer. Tammy had Mary Ruth and Caleb meet her wonderful grandfather, Pastor Ben Wylie. What a great pastor he was! He taught Caleb, Mary Ruth and Tammy many things about what the Bible meant in the next few years.

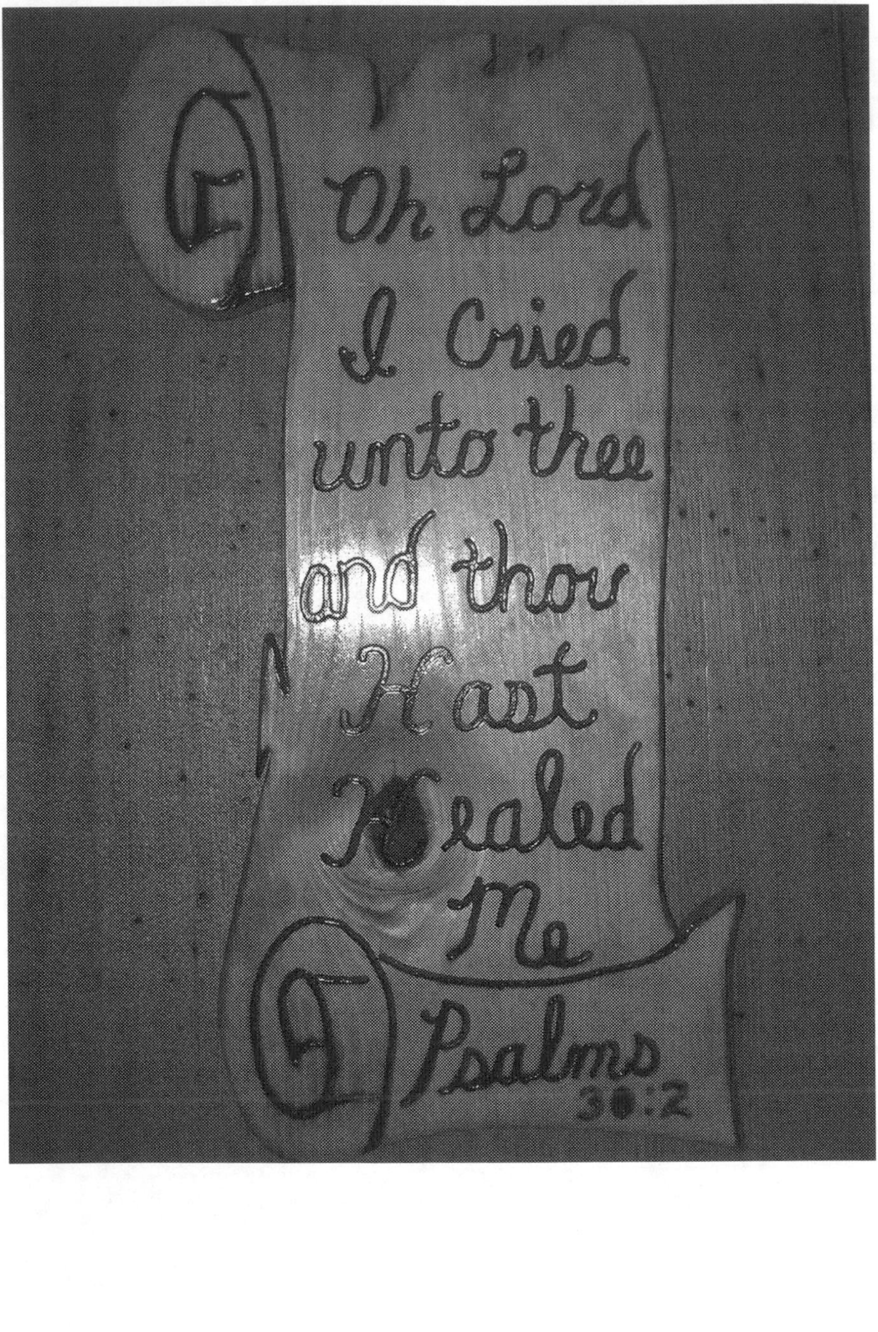
Oh Lord
I Cried
unto thee
and thou
Hast
Healed
Me
Psalms
30:2

Chapter 5

The next five years passed quickly. Caleb was now sixteen years old and in eleventh grade. Mary Ruth was thirteen and in eighth grade in Junior High. She was still best friends with Tammy. They still had all their other friends and the Bible studies. They were learning and teaching others more and more about the Lord. They prayed that they would do His will and walk in His path of righteouness. They loved everyone and always helped them. It seemed like the only person they couldn't get through to was the boy named Mike. He was one of the three that had beaten Caleb up five years ago. Mike was always saying bad things about Caleb and Mary Ruth and they were all lies. Most children didn't listen to Mike, but there were a few that did and stayed with him.

Len was still in the same condition and staying at the nursing home. Everyone still visited him and brought him over to Jane and Josh's home for the holidays. The kids still visited him everyday and prayed for his recovery. Len thanked God that he was still alive and also prayed for his recovery.

Sandy still visited him, but not everyday. She and Paul became good friends and did things together. Paul now had his own little house in St. Cloud. Two bedrooms and one bath, but it was a very nice home.

Two years previously, Thelma and Tom got married and Tom moved to St. Cloud into Thelma's lakefront home. They were a wonderful couple and had a wonderful wedding. Caleb and Mary Ruth now looked at Tom as their grandfather. They loved each other so much. They were all so happy.

Al still came down and visited everyone. He always said to them, "If you need a plane ride, let me know, I'll be glad to help you."

Sandy still loved Len so much! She was so sad that their marriage didn't work out for them. In fact, neither of them mentioned it. She still wore her engagement ring.

Thelma and Tom went to Tammy's grandfather's church a few times with the kids. He was a really great pastor. He gave wonderful sermons. Thelma knew he was teaching the kids and was very thankful for it.

The first time she met him and shook his hand, something tingeled inside of her. It was something that never happened to her before. She couldn't stop thinking of him, or the way he looked, but after awhile it left her mind.

One day she was visiting Jane. Josh and Tom decided to go fishing on the lake. Jane and Thelma were sitting at the table talking. Thelma happened to notice a book that was sitting on the counter. It sort of looked familiar to her.

"Jane, what is that book up there on your counter?"

"Oh, remember the journal Sandy had brought back from that island they were stranded on? I found it in a drawer upstairs and decided to read it again. Last time I read it, I was very emotional because Sandy, the kids, and the men had just gotten home, so I decided to take my time and read it slowly this time. I'm just about finished it. It is a very interesting story."

Thelma asked, "Can I read it when you're finished with it?"

"Of course. As soon as I'm finished, I'll bring it over to you."

"Thank you, I'm really looking forward to reading it." Thelma didn't know why she wanted to read it again but she kept having a feeling to do it.

Len was feeling fine but still unable to move after all these years. He still had a lot of his friends from the police department also visit him. They would tell him about everything that was going on in the community. It was so nice when he had visitors.

This afternoon after Caleb and Mary Ruth left, Sandy showed up. Paul was with her. Len could see how really close they were; after all, they work in the same place. He thought, Should I tell Sandy to forget about me and find a new boyfriend? But I still do have complete faith that God will heal me when it is time. I still pray and I know that everyone else is praying for me. It's also amazing how Caleb and Mary Ruth are closer to the Lord. I have to keep my faith and never give up!

The next morning at 9 AM, a man came into his room and right behind him appeared Dr. Blankenship.

"Hi Len, I want to introduce you again to Dr. Jerald Yost, from New York. If you can remember, he examined you five years ago and told you if he comes across something that might work; he would try to help you. This is now the time.

Len smiled and said, "Thank you. It would be so wonderful if I could be helped after all these years."

Dr. Yost squeezed his hand. "I have to let you know that we have tried this on 52 people. Only two of them recovered. We are constantly trying to improve our procedure. Are you willing to try it?"

"You bet I am!" Len cried out.

"Great I will start the treatment today and teach Dr. Blankenship how to do it and he will teach the nurses. I have to be in London tomorrow. I hope it works, but it will take awhile if it does. Okay, let's go!"

Dr. Yost did his procedures and taught Dr. Blankenship. When he was finished, he squeezed Len's hand again and said, "I hope this works out for you. Nice to meet you, I surely hope this helps you recover."

Len smiled and said. "Thank you so very much for remembering me after all these years and coming down to help me. I'm very thankful to you."

Len didn't tell anyone what was going on. About a month later, Caleb, Mary Ruth, and her friend, Tammy, were visiting Len. They all talked awhile, and then prayed for Len. As they were about to leave, Tammy triped on something that was on the floor and fell unto Len in his wheelchair. For some reason, the wheelchair fell over and Len and Tammy both hit the floor. Len pushed himself up and tried to help Tammy with his arms. He wasn't able to help her, but he did move his back and both his arms.

He didn't even realize what he did until Mary Ruth cried, "Len, you moved your arms!" Len looked at his arms and was able to move them a little bit!

Caleb cried, "Come on Tammy and Mary Ruth; let's get Len back in his wheelchair!" They lifted him and put him back in the wheelchair.

Tammy squeezed his right hand. "Len, do you feel anything?"

"I do!" Len cried.

Tammy and Mary Ruth held Len's hands and Caleb put hands on his ankles. They got on their knees.

Caleb prayed, "DEAR LORD, WE PRAY THAT THE TIME FOR LEN'S RECOVERY IS HERE. WE KNOW, DEAR LORD, THAT YOU ARE HAVING THIS HAPPEN. WE ARE SO VERY THANKFUL AND PRAISE YOU. WE DIDN'T KNOW AT ALL HOW LONG IT WOULD TAKE LEN TO RECOVER, BUT WE KNOW THAT HE IS IN THE RIGHT WAY NOW. WE THANK YOU WITH ALL OUR HEART AND SOUL. YOU ARE OUR WONDERFUL LORD! IN JESUS HOLY NAME, AMEN"

They stood up and hugged Len. Mary Ruth said, "I'm going to run out and tell the nurse what happened!"

She ran out to the nurse and told her. The nurse smiled and cried, "Did it really happen!"

"Come to Len's room and see for yourself!"

The nurse went into the room with Mary Ruth. As she walked over to Len, he lifted up both of his hands a couple of inches.

The nurse cried, "This is truly a miricle that you moved both your hands. It's been years since you've moved. We really didn't think that this would ever happen! I'm going to call Dr. Blankenship and have him come over and check you. He'll be amazed!"

She ran out and called the doctor. He answered the phone and she told him the great news.

"What! This is truly hard to believe. I really didn't think that this would work on Len after all these years! I'll be over as soon as possible!" He hung up the phone and thought, if this is true, I know our Lord is with Len!

The kids stayed with Len untill the doctor arrived. Len told them about the treatment he had been getting now that Dr. Yost, the famous doctor from New York, recommended. He said. "I didn't tell anyone about it because I didn't want to get your hopes up, but now I know the Lord had taken care of me and is helping me! Thank You Dear Lord!"

When the doctor arrived, Len showed him how he could slightly move his arms. "I couldn't do it before Tammy tripped into me and I fell out of my wheelchair! By the way, thank you, Tammy!"

Tammy giggled and said, "Your welcome!"

Dr. Blankenship said, "This is so wonderful! Something great is beginning to take place in you! Tomorrow we will do some more testing on you and see what is happening."

Len smiled and had tears of happiness running down his face.

"Now we can tell everyone the great news," said Caleb.

"How about just holding off for a little while, until I can do better. I do believe the Lord is with me," replied Len.

Tammy said, "We truly believe that also. We won't say anything until you say we can." They all hugged him and said, "See you tomorrow!" The kids went home so happy, but didn't say a word about Len's condition to anyone, even Sandy.

Chapter 6

Thelma was sitting at the kitchen table reading the journal from the island, Tom was reading the newspaper.

Thelma stopped reading and said, "You know, when I read this journal the first time, I was amazed that the female tiger was named Princess Thelma. Then as I read further, I was more amazed to read that the baby girl was named Thelma and had a twin brother. Now I'm really amazed also, to see the year this all took place. It happens to be the same year that I was born. Tom, let me tell you my story."

"Go right ahead, I'd love to hear it. We never actually talked much about our previous lives," said Tom.

"I really don't even know where I was born. I do know that when I was a little girl I was in an orphanage. I'm not sure where it was but I do know I was adopted when I was three years old by my new mom and dad. When I was five, we came to the United States on a boat and I lived here all my life.

When I was seventeen, we lived in New Haven, Ct. My dad was an electrician and my mom worked part time at her friend's restaurant, Eddie Apps Pizza. My dad went down to pick her up from work one night and on their way home, they were hit head on by a huge truck and were both killed.

I was in shock and so depressed. As far as relatives were concerned, I did not have any others. I had just finished high school and even though I was very upset, I needed to find a job. I went to the restaurant called, Eddie Apps Pizza, where my mom had worked. They hired me on the spot! They taught me everything. It was a good job. I really liked it. Several boys used to come in a few times a week. One of them had always caught my eye. I thought that he was so cute and also very nice.

One night, he came up to me and asked me if I would like to go on a date with him. Of course, I said, yes. We went out one night and had a great time. We talked a lot. I found out that he was in his second year of collage and he was going to be a doctor someday. His name was Joseph Lewis. To make a long story short, we got married within a year and I helped him as he graduated from collage and started his internship.

We loved each other so much and ended up having just one daughter, who was the wonderful mother of Caleb and Mary Ruth.

I guess I'm talking a little too much, but my main point is, I wonder how I can ever find out where I was born? I do know that we came from Scotland, as my parents told me when I was in my teens. I never asked anything else way back then. I guess I wasn't interested, but now, as I read this journal, I'm very interested! Could I have been that twin baby girl? Even if I was, who could have taken me from the island and where did we go? I surly don't remember anything, also, can I possibly have a twin brother somewhere? Wow, that would really be something! How could we ever find out?"

The kids heard most of the story as they had arrived home as Thelma was telling it to Tom. Caleb said. "We don't know exactly what to do, but we will try anyway we can to help you find out."

"I'll be glad to help you also," replied Tom. "When we were on the island, I read that journal to the kids and I agree with what you want to find out. It might be just a coincidence about the year you were born and your name, but then again, it might be true. What date is your birthday?"

"It's September 5th," Thelma replied.

"Isn't that the same day as the twins birthday and also near Caleb's?" Mary Ruth asked.

"It sure is, I wasn't even paying any attention to the date before. Luckily, I noticed it this time when I was reading," cried Thelma. "We have to tell our friends about this also! I'm sure they will try to help us find out about the past any way they can!"

The next day after school, the kids walked over to the nursing home where Len stayed. When they walked into the room, Len gave them a big smile. The kids ran up and hugged him.

Mary Ruth asked, "How did the tests work out?"

"They were wonderful! The doctor could hardly believe the x-rays! He said, "According to all the tests we ran on you, you might be back to normal in a few months! Something like this very rarely happens after five years. It is truly a miracle! I told my doctor how we all kept our entire faith in the Lord, and now the time is right, and He is curing me!"

"That's right, we will never give up! We will always keep our faith and trust in the Lord! The great healer!" cried Caleb.

"We are so thankful to Him and love Him so much. Our life is to do His will and walk in His path of righteousness. Caleb and I truly gave ourselves to Him and we will do what He tells us to do. He is our everything! He has been with us and has taken care of us our whole life!" stated Mary Ruth.

Caleb said, "One of our purposes is to teach more and more people about Jesus Christ, and have them to be born again. Right now we do have quite a few kids who attend our Bible studies and have accepted Jesus Christ as their Lord and Savior. The older Mary Ruth and I get, the more we want to do for God. We want to help everyone as much as we can."

"You are both such great people and I'm sure your friend, Tammy, is also!"

"She sure is! I don't know if we ever told you that she has a grandfather, Ben Wylie, who is a pastor at a church in Kissimmee. We have gone to church with her many times and his sermons are great. He is also teaching us about the Bible. We understand a lot more since we've been with him. Thank God that Mary Ruth met Tammy and became best friends with her."

"That's for sure!" said Mary Ruth. "Tammy and I are such great friends. The both of us are friends with just about everyone at school too. It's so nice."

"I know you kids are going to have a great future with the Lord. I'm so thankful for how you both prayed for my healing all these years. You truly never gave up. That's having complete love, faith and trust in God!" Caleb and Mary Ruth hugged and kissed him.

"Kids, I know this sounds strange, but I don't want you to tell anyone about my recovery yet. I want to completely surprise everyone, especially Sandy!"

The kids said, "Okay, if that's what you want, we still won't say a word." The kids then left and started walking home.

Caleb said, "Your right about Tammy. She is so smart and truly believes in the Lord. She does help us a lot and I'm so thankful for that. I believe we became friends with her for a special reason."

"Well, I know for sure that she will be my best friend forever. God bless her and her wonderful family. Her grandpa taught us so much. I know our mom and dad would have done the same thing for us if they were here."

"Thank the Lord that they are up in Heaven with Him," stated Caleb. "I still miss them so much, but I'm thankful that we were with them as long as we were."

"I'm so grateful that we have our grandma and her great new husband, Tom, who saved us with Len from the factory in the Bahamas where we were held to work all day with all those other children, who were also saved. I wonder how they are all doing now. I hope they're having a great life."

"Thank God also for Sandy, Jane, Josh and Paul. They all did a lot in our lives. They are all good Christain people who love us as we love them."

They got home, did their home work and had supper with their grandparents. They were on the way to their rooms to read their Bibles. Thelma amd Tom were watching the news from Orlando. As they walked past the TV, they both happened to look at it. There was a boy, who looked about eighteen years old, in handcuffs, being led by the police.

Mary Ruth cried, "Look Caleb!" "That boy looks just like Pepi, the boy who taught us how to work at the factory and helped me when I passed out."

"It sure does look like him! When did he come to the U.S. and why is he being arrested? We have to find out if it is him!"

Mary Ruth said, "I'm sure Paul can find out everything for us. We have his phone number, let's call him!"

Thelma and Tom were listening to what the kids were talking about. Thelma asked, "Do you both really think that is the boy who was held in the factory with you?"

"It certainly looked like him. We're going to call Paul and ask him to check it out for us. We have to find out for sure if it is Pepi and what happened."

Tom said, "He also looks somewhat familiar to me. Go ahead, you know the phone is in the kitchen."

They both ran into to the kitchen. Caleb picked the phone up and dialed Paul's number. Paul picked up his phone and said, "Hello."

"Hi, this is Caleb."

"I'm so glad to hear from you! I haven't seen you and Mary Ruth for awhile. Is everything okay?"

"Everything is fine, but we would like you to do us a favor, if it is possible."

"Sure thing, I'll be glad to help you anyway I can."

Caleb explained to him what they saw on TV, who they thought it might be, and that they wanted to know what happened if it was Pepi.

"No problem. When I go to work tomorrow, I will call the Orlando police department and get all the information."

"Thank you so much, we really appreciate your help and will stop at the police station to see you on our way home tomorrow."

"I will have all the information for you and will be very glad to see you and Mary Ruth. Bye."

Caleb hung up the phone and they went to Mary Ruth's room. Caleb said, "If that is Pepi, we have to help him."

"You bet! He is really a good person."

"Well, we'll find out tomorrow. Good night, Mary Ruth, I love you."

"I love you too, Caleb."

Chapter 7

The next day, Thelma and Tom went over to see Jane and Josh. Thelma told them about all the things she found out in the journal and about her past.

Jane said, "Oh my, that is unbelievable! Who ever thought something like this could have happened to you. It surly sounds like it was you."

"But how will we ever find out about anything more of what happened? That would be very difficult. I wouldn't even know where to start. I'll probably never find out," said Thelma.

"We'll keep trying to think of a way we can find out what happened," replied Josh.

"We'll try to find out as long as we live." stated Tom.

Caleb and Mary Ruth were having lunch with their friends at school. Tammy was with them and they were telling her about what they saw on the news last night, that the boy looked just like a boy, named Pepi, that they were held in the factory with in the Bahamas.

Tammy said, "If you need any help, I'll be glad to be with you."

They also told Tammy how Paul is going to check things out for them and that they should find out this afternoon if it was Pepi.

Then Mary Ruth started telling her about all the things her grandma started to realize after reading the island journal again, but she did not know how to find anything more out to confirm that it was really her that was born on the island.

"That's really something to not know how your life began when you were a baby and to never have known if you had a twin brother. I wish her good luck to find out about her past," replied Tammy.

After school, as always, Caleb and Mary Ruth went to see Len.

He now was even moving a little bit more than yesterday. They were so happy for him and thankful to the Lord.

When they left, they walked down to the police station. Paul was at the front desk. They hugged and kissed each other.

Mary Ruth asked, "Did you check out about that boy who was arrested in Orlando?"

"You bet I did! It is Pepi. Apparently he lives in Orlando and was arrested for trying to rob a gas station. Two of his friends got away, but he was caught by a police officer."

"That just doesn't seem right that he would rob anyone," said Caleb. "I wonder when and why he came to Florida."

"He is still in jail. If he had fifty dollars he could get out on bond, they said."

"We want to help him! What can we do? cried Mary Ruth.

"I would say, first of all, talk to your grandparents. Tell them the whole situation. It would be great if you can somehow get the fifty dollars and get him out of jail. Then he can talk with you all and tell you exactly what happened. Maybe he could stay with you, depending on what's going on in his life. Your grandparents would have to agree first. If all that was able to happen, I can drive you up to Orlando on my day off after you both get out of school."

Mary Ruth said, "That would be great! We'll go talk to our grandparents right now and let you know what's happening."

"Thank you so very much for helping us. We have to get together one of these days and do something."

"Sounds good to me! Don't forget to let me know if you need me to take you to Orlando. Take care, It was great seeing you both again. Bye."

Caleb and Mary Ruth went home and talked with their grandparents. They told them that the boy really was Pepi and what Paul told them they could do for him.

Thelma asked, "Are you sure he's a good person?"

"Definately!" said Mary Ruth, then explained how he more or less saved her life when they were working in the factory.

"That was really wonderful of him to help you like that. Tell you what! I will give you the fifty dollars and you can bring him down here so we can all help him," stated Tom.

Caleb said, "Thank you so much! We want to teach Pepi about Jesus and have him be reborn in Him. Hopefully, things will work out. We're going to call Paul and tell him our plans and find out when his day off is. We love you both and thank you for your help."

They called Paul and explained what they wanted to do. He said, "Great, I'll be off the day after tomorrow, which will be Thursday, and we'll all go to Orlando and and get Pepi out of jail. See you on Thursday. I'll pick you up at school. Bye."

That same night, Tammy and her mom and dad went to Kissimmee to visit her grandparents and have dinner with them.

After dinner, they sat and watched TV for awhile. Tammy started talking to her grandparents, "I want to tell you a story about my best friend, Mary Ruth's grandmother."

She told her grandparents all she could remember, about Thelma reading a journal that Sandy had brought from the island they were stranded on for several months. Her grandpa just looked at her in shock as she told him a lot about what the journal said and that Thelma might be one of the twins. She also told him the name of the father and the twin boy, which was Benjamin and also her grandpa's name.

"This story is very shocking to me! I was never in an orphanage, but I was in Scotland when I was a child. We did move to America when I was five yeas old. There were many other people on that boat with their young children. I remember seeing a little girl who for some reason attracted me. But we never did get to be together or even talk.

We moved to a small town in PA. named Mahanoy City, where a lot of people worked in coal mines nearby. The other end of the town went to a lot of farm country. It was a very nice place. Can you give me Thelma's phone number? I know it sounds strange, but something is telling me that I should talk to her. I don't know anything about being on any island when I was born. I do know that my mom and dad, your great grandparents, still live in PA. I wish they would move down here but they want to stay in PA. That means that we don't get to see them very often, thank God that they are living so long. Like I said, something is just telling me that I should talk to Thelma."

"Her phone number is, 412-4770," said Tammy.

"I will call her tomorrow," said her grandpa.

Tammy's dad said, "We have to get going. Tammy has some homework to do before she goes to bed. Take care, we love you both so much! See you on Sunday."

They drove home. As they were driving, Tammy's mom asked, "I wonder why he wants to talk to Thelma?"

"I really feel that for some reason, the Lord told me to tell him that story," stated Tammy.

The next day, Pastor Ben did call Thelma. She answered the phone and he introduced himself.

Thelma said, "Believe me, I truly remember meeting you and being at several of your wonderful church services."

Pastor Wylie told Thelma how Tammy told him about how she read a journal that Sandy had brought back from an island. He said, "I don't know why, but for some reason, I want to talk to you about this. I'm sure that this is the Lord telling me to do this."

"I'll be home all day today so your more than welcomed to come over any time you can."

"I have a pretty quiet day today. Tammy also wrote your address down with your phone number. How about I come over around two o'clock?"

"That will be fine. See you soon. Bye."

Pastor Ben arrived exactly at 2 PM. He knocked on the door and Thelma answered. They both smiled at each other and for some reason, instead of shaking hands, they hugged each other. They both thought to themselves, What made me do that? They went into the living room and sat down on the couch.

Ben said, "The reason I'm here, I guess, is because last night Tammy told me your story, about how reading the journal affected you. You think you might have been born on that island and you were a twin?"

Thelma told him the whole story and said that if he wants to, he can take the journal home and read it.

"Thanks, I'll be glad to read it, but I don't know why. Just because my name is Benjamin? I surly doubt that I could have been born there. My parents and I are from Scotland." Thelma didn't mention that she was also.

For some reason, Thelma and Ben never thought to ask each other when their birthday was.

"It's been so nice talking to you and I will return the journal as soon as I finish reading it. I think it will be very interesting. Of course, if there is any way I can help you to find more out about your past, I'll be glad to. Right now, I don't have any idea what to do except pray to the Lord that someday you will find out about your past."

"Thank you so much, Pastor Wylie. It certainly has been nice talking to you. See you soon!" Pastor Wylie got in his car and headed back to Kissimmee.

When the Pastor got home, he sat down on the couch and started reading the journal. When he got about a third of the way through, his wife, Gloria, got home from grocery shopping. He got up and helped her put the groceries away and told her about going to see Thelma and that she gave him the journal to read.

He said, "I'm only about a third of the way through the journal, but it's very interesting. After supper I'm going to start reading it again. Something is telling me to read it all as soon as I can."

Around 9 pm, Ben was just about at the end of the journal, when all the people except Kathleen and Ben were taken from the island. It was so sad how they were alone on the island without their children. Thelma did tell him that Caleb and Mary Ruth found the bones in the cave and how they buried them and prayed for them. It was interesting to also read it. When he finished the book, something was still telling him to read it again. He looked through it again and thought, I have to look at the names of the doctor and his wife. My father was a doctor. Is that just a coincidence? He looked it up again and was in shock. He didn't even pay attention to the names before, but his dad's name is Ken and his mom's name is Lynn, but they had a different last name. The last name in the journal was Davidson, but their name is Wylie.

He told Gloria the situation. Gloria said, "Wow, this is shocking! The good news is that your mom and dad are still alive in PA. You have to get in touch with them and ask if any of this journal is true. Just pray that they will tell you the truth. There might be something that they never wanted you to know. If it is true, that means Thelma might be your twin sister!"

"You know, when I met her the first time, for some reason, we both hugged each other. There is something drawing us together."

"I'm going to call my mom and dad right now!" Ben dialed the number and his mom answered the phone. "Hi mom, it's Ben, how are you doing?"

"I'm doing fine Ben, you just talked to us yesterday."

"I know I did, but something has come up and I want to talk to you and dad and find out if either of you know anything about it."

"What are you talking about Ben?"

"It's about an island in the Caribbean and some people from Scotland that were living there quite a while ago. Did you ever hear of anything like that?"

Ben's mom didn't say anything.

"Mom, are you there?"

"Yes Ben, I heard what you said. Let me put your dad on the phone."

Ben's dad said, "Hi, is something wrong? Your mom looks pale all of a sudden."

"No, nothing is wrong. I was just asking mom if she ever heard of some people from Scotland who were living on a southern Caribbean island." Now his dad didn't say anything.

"What is going on with the two of you?"

"Ben, it's a long story, we really don't want to talk about it!"

"Why, did you know those people? I want to hear the whole story in person. I'm going to drive up to see you. I'll be there the day after tomorrow. I can only stay for a couple of days but I want to hear the whole story and I want it to be the truth. I will see you soon. I love you both so much and I know you will tell me everything."

"Okay son, we'll see you soon and we'll tell you the whole truth. You have a right to know. Bye bye."

Ben hung up the phone, went in the living room, and just stared at Gloria. "Gloria, go pack a suitcase for us. We're leaving for PA. tomorrow."

"What? Are your parents sick?"

"No, they're fine." He told Gloria about the conversation they just had, and what happened.

Gloria was shocked. "It will be very interesting to hear what they have to say!"

"You bet it will! We'll leave early in the morning and probably spend the night in Virginia, then get to mom and dad's early in the afternoon the next day."

"I'm really looking forward to it!"

Ben called the church to let them know that he would be gone for a few days. He told them that if for any reason he couldn't get back by Sunday, he would let them know and they should call his friend, Sam Lynch. He is a retired minister and he would preach a sermon for them on Sunday.

Chapter 8

The next morning they left and headed up I 95 to PA. The traffic was not bad. When they finally got to Virginia, they stayed over night in a hotel, had breakfast in the morning, then continued driving to PA.

At 1:30 pm they arrived at Ben's parent's home. Ben knocked on the door. His mom and dad both answered it. They all hugged and kissed each other.

His dad said, "We're so glad to see you again, although we don't want to tell you this story."

"But it is your right to know the truth," his mom replied. Ben and Gloria just looked at each other.

"Come on, have a seat on the couch in the living room." They sat down and his mom got them some ice tea.

Ben said, "Go ahead, whenever your ready, you can start the story. By the way, I do have the journal with me in case you would want to read it and see what Kathleen wrote and what might have happened to them."

"We would love to read it and yes, the names of the doctor and nurse, I am sure were our names. We did change our last name. Okay, here goes!"

"We did leave Scotland with several other couples, who were our good friends, in 1902. We got on a hugh ship and headed for a beautiful island in the Caribbean where no one else lived. We took everything we needed including animals because we weren't very sure if anything would be there to help us. We took tons of seeds and planted them when we got there. We build homes and a church. We led a good life and really enjoyed it, which was good because we were stranded there, as our ship was taken away in a storm. I was the only doctor and your mom and I helped everyone with their physical problems. We delivered Kathleen and Ben's twins. They were perfect and beautiful and had no problems at all. When they were a few monthes old, your mom offered to watch the twins whenever they wanted to take a walk with their pet tigers. Your mom never had any problems with the babies, they were so sweet. We both loved them."

"We will never ever forget what happened one day. Your mom was taking care of the babies, who were now about six monthes old, and I happened to be in the house with her. All of a sudden, a big bunch of pirates entered our village. They all had guns and made everyone come outside. I carried the baby named Thelma, and your mom carried Ben. We were all in shock. We had no idea what was going to happen to us. They all had guns pointed at us. We thought that they were just going to kill us. I know we were all praying to the Lord in our minds. They then led us to their small row boats and took us all to their ship. They put us in rooms and locked the doors."

Mom started talking, "She said, "Your dad and I were so very worried about the babies. What are they going to eat? We had no milk or anything else to give them."

"We laid the babies on the bed, got down on our knees, and prayed to God for help for all of us, especially the babies and all the other children."

"We felt the boat starting to move and knew that we were leaving the island. Where were we going? What are they going to do with us? The babies were getting hungry, but there was nothing we could do for them. About five hours later, we heard the door unlock. The babies were both crying. One of the pirates came in and gave us some food. Your mom just looked at him and said, "What about the babies? If they don't at least get some milk, they will die."

The pirate said, "Sorry, we don't have milk, I guess they will die," then left the room. Your mom and I both started crying and again prayed to the Lord. We had complete faith in Him, that He would somehow, someway, help the babies."

"About half an hour later, the door unlocked again. It was the same pirate that was there before and he had one of our friends with him. Her name was Ellen Hopkins. He then locked the door and left her with us. We both hugged her. I asked, "Why did he bring you here?"

Ellen replied, "I heard them talking about the babies, that they were going to die because there was no milk to give them. The one man said, "We'll just throw them off the boat. I'm sure the sharks are hungry." They all laughed. I was in shock. When the pirates came in my room, I told them how I could help the babies. That's why he brought me here."

Your mom asked her, "How can you possibly help the babies?"

"No one on the island, except my husband knew this. I still breast feed my three year old son, Scott."

"We both grabbed her, kissed her, and thanked her so much for doing this for the babies. We then praised and thanked God for saving the babies."

"For the next few days, the pirate would bring Ellen back several times each day and the babies were doing okay.

One day, when Ellen came to our room, she told us what her husband heard the pirates talking about when he went to the bathroom. Apparently, for some unknown reason, they are taking us to Spain and are going to sell all of us as slaves. That was hard to believe, but it was true. What are we going to do?

When we finally got to Spain, we all got sold. Luckily, your mom, I and the babies, got sold to the same very rich people. We have no idea who all the others were sold to.

They took us to their beautiful house and they showed us where we would stay at night. The problem was, they only spoke Spanish. We did not understand at first what they were telling us to do and they had no idea what we were saying. They did give us food in the kitchen and even baby bottles full of milk for the twins. There were also little pieces of food that the babies were able to eat. We thanked God that we were now doing fine.

Instead of telling us what to do, they would show us and of course we would do whatever they desired. They even gave us a playpen to put the babies in while we worked.

We were there for about two months when their daughter came home from college. When she met us, she smiled at us, but when she saw the babies, she picked them both up and hugged them.

Later that night, after her parents went to bed, she came over to our bedroom and knocked on the door. We opened it and in English she said, "May I come in? My name is Carman."

I said, "Of course." We introduced ourselves to her.

She just looked at us and the babies and asked, "How did you become slaves with two babies?"

We told her all that happened to us.

She said, "Oh no! My mom and dad would not have bought you if they knew that!"

"Thank God they did buy us! We're doing fine here with them. We are very lucky! We could have all been bought by different people and might never have seen each other again'" replied your mom.

I told her how I was a doctor and your mom was a nurse.

She said, "Wow, now you are house cleaners and slaves."

After we got done talking, she said, "If you or the babies need anything, let me know. I will only be here for two weeks, then I have to go back to college."

We thanked her and she left. She was a very nice and loving girl.

A few days later, as your mom and I were cleaning in the kitchen, Carman ran into the kitchen and screamed. "Please help us! I think my dad just died!"

We ran into the living room, took him off the chair, and laid him flat on the floor. I checked him and he had no pluse. Your mom yelled to Carman to call for help! We started giving him CPR. Before the ambulance arrived, we kept checking his pluse. Finally, it started beating again.

Carman and her mother were crying. When we told them his pluse was beating, they hugged each other and held his hands. Just then, the ambulance arrived. They checked his pulse, it still was doing okay, picked him up, and put him in the ambulance. Carman and her mom jumped in with them.

They came home that night and they both hugged and kissed us. Carman's mom went to her room, but Carman stayed and thanked us again. She told us that her dad was doing fine. They are now testing his heart to try to find out what happened. They told her that he did have a heart attack. She told the doctor what we did when his heart had stopped beating. The doctor told her and her mother that if we didn't do the CPR on your dad, he never would have lived until the ambulance got there.

She said, "If it wasn't for you and your wife my father would be dead.

He's only forty three years old! My mother and I are so very thankful and grateful to you. I'm going to do something for you. I have to talk to my mom and we will decide.

I said, "Don't worry, we are also thankful that he is okay and we thank the Lord that we were here to help him."

Carman replied, "I did tell my dad how you both saved his life and also that you are a doctor and a nurse. I told my parents a little bit about why you were sold as slaves. My dad and mom are so thankful that you were here to save my dad, but they were so sad about what happened to you all and how you got here."

For the next week, Carman's mom was so good to us. She bought us and the babies a whole bunch of clothes, shoes, underwear and even bought me a wallet and your mom a purse."

My mom said, "We thought, we surly needed many of the things they bought us all and we were so thankful, but I thought, why would they buy us a wallet and a purse? We don't go anywhere and we don't have anything to put in them. We thought that they were just extremily nice to us.

The babies were getting bigger and stronger and able to eat more food. Their teeth were starting to come in. They were so sweet and we loved them so much."

Dad continued the story. "A few days later, Carman's dad came home from the hospital and was doing fine. He hugged us and thanked us for saving his life.

The next day, Carman and her parents came up to us. They asked us to come and sit in the living room with them.

Carman said, "We all had a talk together and truly decided how we are going to thank you for saving my dad. My dad really made the decision. We are going to give you money, we have bought you a trip on a ship to take you back to Scotland. We bought suitecases for you to pack your clothes in and you all will be leaving the day after tomorrow. We hate to see you leave us, but you truly earned it."

Your mom and I hugged each other and cried. We ran over and hugged and kissed Carman and her parents.

I said, "Thank you so much, we are so thankful to you.! We love you!"

Carman said, "We love you so much also! You can now go back to what you were doing, but don't forget to get ready for your trip! I'm only kidding, I know you won't forget! Tomorrow, I'm taking my parents to see if we can find some people to take your place. I'm sure we will never find anyone as wonderful as you all are, but we'll do our best. We will truly miss your babies! By the way, we'll be leaving at 9 AM the day after tomorrow to get to the ship, so make sure that your ready."

"Your dad and I were so very happy! We went back to the kitchen, got down on our knees, praised and thanked the Lord for helping us. We knew that it was through Him that this came about and this was the time!

After we were finished for the day, we went back to our room, there were two suitcases there and on our bed, a large amount of money. We were completely shocked when we counted it. We knew that this family was rich, but we were still completely stunned! We knew that this money would tremendously help us in Scotland. We were so excited! We picked the babies up, hugged them and danced in happiness with them.

The next day we did as much as possible to take care of the house. Later on, Carman and her parents returned home. Carman told us that they did find some very nice people to come and work for them. They would be coming the day after we leave.

Chapter 9

The next day, we were taken to the port, where the ship was. It was a beautiful ship and again, we thanked them for everything. We got on the ship and they showed us to our cabin. It was a lovely room with a port window. We were able to look out and see the ocean. All our meals were given to us. It was like a vacation.

It only took three days to get to Scotland. We got off the boat and hugged and kissed the babies. We finally returned to our home land!

We went inside the building that took care of the people who arrived. I asked them if I could please use their phone. I called my friend, Earl, hoping that he would be home. He answered the phone and I told him who it was. He was very surprised to hear me.

He said, "I thought you were on an island in the Caribbean? We haven't heard from you for ages. We prayed that you were all right."

I said, "It's a truly long story. I will tell it to you and you will be very shocked when you hear what happened. My wife is with me and two twin babies."

Earl asked, "You mean you had babies while you were on the island?"

"I will talk to you about it later, okay? Is there any chance that we can stay at your house for a few days until we can find a place of our own? We'll be living here again.

No problem! Phyllis and I will be very glad to see you again. Where are you? We'll come and pick you up.

I told him where we were and he said, That's fine, I know where it is. It will take us awhile to get there, but we will be there. Just relax. We can't wait to see you again!

About two hours later, Earl and Phyllis showed up. We all ran to each other, hugged, kissed, and cried. We were so glad to see each other again!

They said, Oh, what beautiful babies you have! They were truly attracted to them.

When we got to their house, we had a great lunch and they showed us to our room. Then we sat down with them and your mom and I basically told them the story of what happened.

They also were good friends of Ben and Kathleen and were very upset to hear what happened to them.

Are they still on the island?

As far as I know, they might be.

I have a friend who has a good sized boat. I wonder if we can rescue them, if they might still be alive? If he can take us down there, we can search the island, providing that the pirates aren't there. I will get in touch with him tomorrow and ask if he would be able to do it.

When we went to bed that night, we were so very thankful to God that we were there. The next day, we went to a real estate place that sold homes. Your mom and I told them what we were looking for, we talked with them and they told us what was available

We looked at several houses and were getting tired. None of them were what we wanted. Finally we were looking at the seventh house. Your mom said that this will be the last one for today.

It seemed like a very nice neighborhood and the home was perfect for us. The price wasn't bad and we had more than enough money to buy it. We told the man that this was it and we will come back tomorrow to talk with him about it.

We went back to Earl's home. He and Phyllis were amazed that we found a home so quickly and they knew the neighborhood was a very good one.

Phyllis then said, We'll be glad to help you shop for all the things you will be needing for your new home. How long will it be until you move in?

I told them that we would be paying cash for the home and I'm sure we'll be moving in about a week. Now we had to get going and start buying all the things for our new home.

The next day, after we went to the realtor, we all went shopping. Earl and I decided to go into a store that sold bathroom products, as the bathroom needed some replacements. I was carrying Thelma and I asked Phyllis to hold her while Earl and I went into the store for a few minutes. Your mom was holding Ben.

While your mom and Phylliswere outside waiting for us, a couple came up to them.

Mom said, They walked up to us, looked at the babies and smiled. The woman said, What lovely children you have. I said, Thank you. Suddenly, they hit us both on the head with something. Phyllis and I fell down, they grabbed both the children and ran down the street.

A few seconds later, your dad and Earl came out of the store and saw us laying on the pavement. As they ran to us, I screamed and cried, A couple took the babies and ran down the street!

They both took off after them. They didn't see anyone. All of a sudden, they seen a woman carrying a baby go around a corner. Your dad and Earl ran after her. As Earl was running he triped on something that was on the payment and fell down. Your dad kept on running and he caught the woman. The first thing your dad did was grab the baby and the woman took off running. She then jumped in a car with the man and the other baby and they took off.

Earl came limping around the corner. Your dad handed the baby to him and ran as fast as he could after the car the couple was in, but there was no way he could catch them.

He came back to Earl crying, He hugged the baby, which was Ben. The couple had gotten away with Thelma.

They ran back to Phyllis and me. We were now able to stand up. I seen that he only had one of the babies. I cried, Where is Thelma!!

He told us how they took off with her. I was crying and your dad had tears running down his cheeks. He said, We have to get to the police and tell them what happened and hope that they will be able to catch them. We got to the police station and your dad told them what just happened to us and what the car looked like that they took off in.

They sent two police men to quickly take off and find them. They actually did find them about two hours later. They were going up a large mountain. The police were chasing them. As the kidnappers were going around a curve, they were going so fast, that they missed the turn and went over the cliff and into the ocean.

A few days later, they found the couples bodies, but said that the baby might have floated away or maybe was eaten by a shark. We were so upset! We loved Thelma so much and now she was dead!

Gloria and I just stared at each other when they told us what happened to little Thelma!

Dad spoke again, We were so sad but so thankful that we still had Ben. We prayed to the Lord that Thelma was now up in Heaven with Him, and thanked the Lord that we were able to save Benjamin.

A few days later, we were still at Earl's home and didn't really get anything for our new house because we were so upset.

Finally, I said to your mom, We must thank the Lord that He saved us and had us save Ben. We must lead a good and loving life and help others with all their needs.

We finally bought all the things that we needed for the house and moved in. Your mom and I opened up a doctor's office and took care of many people, including the poor and the needy who didn't have any money to go to a doctor's when they were sick, especially, little children. Your mom never was able to get pregnant and we were so thankful that we had you!

We went to church every Sunday and you, Ben, went to Sunday school. You learned about the Lord. We all prayed together every night. We never told you about your twin sister and how she died or anything about our adventure. We felt that it would only make you upset.

When Ben was five years old, we decided to move to America. We had heard so much about how wonderful that country was. We sold our house, said goodbye to everyone and sailed to America. Before we left, we talked many more doctors into helping the poor and the needy, which they all agreed to do.

When we arrived in America, we went to PA. and got a home in Scranton. You basically know the rest. Of course you know that the Ben I talked about is you! What do you think? Should we have told you about all of this before?"

Ben said, "Of course I knew that the Ben you were talking about is me!" Ben then told them that he loved them with all his heart and thanked them for everything they did for him, especially for saving him when he was a baby. "It is because of you both that I became a pastor. I also understand why you didn't want me to know all of the things that happened when I was a child. I truly love the Lord with all my heart. I will always love you and consider you my parents. Did you adopt me?"

Mom said, "No, everyone thought that you were our own child, so we just kept you with us. We are so sad that Thelma was never found. The police tried to find her body for a long time but never found it. I wonder what she would be like today if she had lived? We'll never know and we're sorry that you can't be with your twin sister."

Ben asked, "Were my real parents Kathleen and Ben, the couple that was left on the island? From reading the journal, I kind of know what became of them. You will know more after you read the journal."

Ben's dad said, "Everything I told you was the complete truth. Kathleen and Ben are your real parents."

Ben replied, "I figured that they were my real parents. Speaking of the truth, you are going to be shocked when you hear my story!"

"Quite awhile ago, I met a lady at my church. Her grandchildren, Caleb and Mary Ruth Powell, are best friends with your great granddaughter, Tammy. Those two kids are the ones that were stranded on the island with Sandy and a few men about five years ago. I will tell you about that story later.

When I met their grandmother, something just drew me to her. I had no idea why. Now, I'm just about positive why! Her name is Thelma! She is my age and from Scotland. I have to find out her date of birth to make sure, but I just know that she is my twin sister!"

Ben's mom and dad nearly fainted. His dad asked, "How could this be possible? We thought that she was up in Heaven with the Lord all these years!"

Ben replied, "The Lord has brought us together for a reason and I'm so thankful that He did!"

His mom and dad hugged and kissed him. They were sobbing of happiness. Mom said, "We are also very thankful to the Lord if this is really true! How wonderful this is, to know that she might have been alive all these years and hopefully had a good life!"

"When we go back to Florida, I have to tell Thelma this story. She will be so happy to realize that I am her twin brother. I also promise to make an arrangement for Gloria and I to bring her up here to meet you, or have you both come down to Florida to meet her. If you come down, you can also meet Thelma's grandchildren, Caleb and Mary Ruth, and most of the people who were stranded on the island with them. I want you to read the journal first, especially the ending. Then I will tell you what I know of Caleb and Mary Ruth's living on the island. If you come down, Thelma and the kids can tell you everything that happened to each of them and you can tell Thelma what happened to her when she was a baby. You and Thelma will be stunned!"

"We certainly want to come down to Floria and meet all of them," stated dad.

"We always wondered why we were living so long. Now we know that the Lord wants us to be with Thelma again! We can"t wait!" cried mom.

"Lets have supper then you can tell us what you know had happened on the island. Tomorrow your mom and I are looking forward to reading the journal."

They had a delicious supper and then talked for quite awhile. Dad said, "Come to think of it, I remember seeing on the news that some people, including two children, were on a plane coming to Florida and just disappeared. Was that them?"

"You bet it was!"

"Wow, just think, they were Thelma's grandchildren!" cried dad.

Mom replied, "Wait a minute, I also remember something like a tornado, hitting a theater in St. Cloud. Was that them also?"

"It sure was!"

"This is kind of unbelievable!"

"The Lord is always with these two children. I must also say that I'm sure He watches over Tammy also. I think that is the reason they became such good friends. You both know that Tammy has been through many problems also. Well, it's getting pretty late. Lets all go and have a good sleep."

Before they went to bed, they all held hands and praised and thanked the Lord for all the wonderful things they just found out.

The next morning after breakfast, Ben's parents read the journal. Dad said, "Boy, what a book! We never even knew that Kathleen was keeping a journal. It is so sad, whatever happened to them. They missed their children so much. I wish they were able to know that your mom and I were taking care of them. We didn't even know that there was a cave on the island. I wonder what happened to their pet tigers?"

"You probably will be more surprised when you talk to Caleb and Mary Ruth. They will tell you what happened to them on the island."

"We are so looking forward to meeting them all," said mom.

"If you want to, you can leave with us tomorrow and I can drive you home whenever you want to go back."

"I'm sure we can do that. We really don't have a lot to do these days at our age and we are truly looking forward to going with you."

Gloria said, "That's great! I will help you pack today and tomorrow we'll all be on our way!"

"That's wonderful! We are so thankful to the Lord and so excited!"

Chapter 10

Caleb and Mary Ruth went to school on Thursday. They were truly looking forward to seeing Pepi again. At lunch time they told Tammy that hopefully they were going to get him out of jail today and that Paul was going to take them up to the Orlando jail after school.

Mary Ruth told Tammy that their grandpa gave them the money to bail Pepi out of the jail.

"Boy, that is really nice of him to help Pepi. I hope Pepi is doing okay and remembers who you both are," said Tammy.

Caleb replied, "I'm sure he will. We're going to bring him back to our house if he will agree to it."

"Good luck. I will pray to God to help you."

"Thank you, Tammy." They went back to class.

After school, Paul was there to pick them up. The kids got into the car and they drove to the Orlando police station. They all went inside.

Paul told Caleb and Mary Ruth to go and sit down while he talks to the police officer.

Paul introduced himself and told them that he was a police officer from St. Cloud. He told the officer that he wanted to get Pepi out of jail and he would be responsible for him to come back to court. He paid him the fifty dollars.

The officer said, "Okay, just have a seat and we'll have him up here in a few minitues, then he can leave with you."

One of the other officers went back to Pepi's cell and opened the door. He said, "Follow me, you'll be getting out of jail today."

Pepi just looked at him. He asked, "How could this be happening?"

The officer replied, "A police officer from St. Cloud is here to take you."

Pepi thought, How can that be? I was never even in St. Cloud. Why would an officer be here to get me out of jail?

Pepi followed the officer. When they came up to the desk, Pepi just looked around. All of a sudden, he saw a boy and girl jump up and run over to him. He immediately recognized them! They hugged each other and cried. They all were so happy to see each other again.

Mary Ruth said, "Pepi, we missed you and always wondered what became of you."

"We're here to help you like you helped us when we were prisoners at the factory. You'll be coming and staying at our house until you go to court."

Pepi was in shock, but so happy. Caleb introduced him to Paul, their wonderful friend, who brought them here.

Pepi said, "You must be the police officer fron St. Cloud!"

"I sure am!" replied Paul. "I'm so glad to meet you. You were so good to Caleb and Mary Ruth in the past. Let's get in the car and go back to St. Cloud. You can tell us what happened and why you were arrested."

They got in the car and headed for St. Cloud. Pepi said, "I will tell you the whole story and it will be the truth, I promise. I will not lie!"

"Go ahead, we're listening."

Pepi stated, "Later I will tell you the story of how I got here and why I am alone, but first I will tell you why I was arrested. There are two guys that I know, their not good people. I always tried my best to stay away from them. A few nights ago, I was sitting on the steps, by myself, at the apartment I was staying at with some friends.

A few minutes later, Howard and Lee came by. They sat down on each side of me. I thought, Oh no, now what?

Howard said, Pepi, we need you to do us a little favor. We are heading for a gas station down the street. Unfortunately, we need some money and it's the only way we can get some.

I asked, What do you mean by that? Are you and Lee going to rob the place?

You shouldn't say that. We just need some money and we need you to help us, said Lee.

I said, No way am I getting involved with you! Next thing I knew, Howard pulled a gun out of his pocket and said, Unless you don't want to die, you will help us or I'll shot you in your head.

I knew that he really meant it! They are two weird guys! Okay, I said, just put your gun away. What do you want me to do?

All we want you to do is go around the cash register, hold the worker, while I'm pulling the money out of the register and Lee is standing and watching at the front door of the station. It isn't hard. Can you do this for us? You won't get any of the money, but at least you'll live.

Howard was still holding the gun. I said, Sure, no problem, just don't shoot me.

Okay, let's go, Lee said. Howard put the gun back in his pocket. We walked a few blocks to the gas station. There were no cars there, so we went inside.

Lee stood at the front door, holding it shut. Howard took his gun out and pointed it at the employee. I ran back and put my arms around him. Howard put his gun back in his pocket and started empting the cash register.

All of a sudden, Lee yelled, Let's get out of here! A police car just pulled up for some reason.

As Lee and Howard started running, I let go of the man I was holding and was going to start running also, but the man turned around and punched me in the face. I fell down on the floor. Just then, the police officer came in the door. He had no idea that a robbery had just taken place. Then he heard the employee yell, Help! The office ran over, pulled his gun out and arrested me for the crime.

I couldn't believe it! To think that Howard and Lee were the ones robbing the place, they got away, and I was arrested. I tried to tell the officer why I was there, but he told me to shut up, and took me to jail. They won't believe a word I say."

"It's hard for police officers to believe anyone that is caught doing a robbery. We have a lot of people lie to us," Paul replied.

"I understand, but the truth is that I never commited a crime before and the only reason I was there was because they were going to kill me if I didn't help them."

"We will try to help you in anyway we can," stated Caleb.

Paul said, "Me too!"

"We have a lot of talking to do together. We can tell you all the things that happened to us in the last six years and you can tell us your stories," said Mary Ruth.

They finally got to their home in St. Cloud and they all went in. Caleb introduced Pepi to his grandparents. Right away Pepi recognized Tom, who rescued him from the factory with a man named Len.

"We're so very glad to meet you," Thelma said. She and Tom both hugged him.

"Supper is ready. Paul, we would love to have you to join us." They all sat down at the table, thanked God for the food, and had a wonderful meal.

After supper, Paul thanked Thelma and Tom and told the kids to keep in touch with him. I will also have to check on you everyday, Pepi. It was nice meeting you. Whatever you do, don't get in any kind of trouble." Paul then went to his house.

Caleb, Mary Ruth and Pepi went out on the back porch and talked for awhile. Pepi was amazed to hear some of the things that Caleb and Mary Ruth had been through.

Mary Ruth said, "The Lord was always with us and took care of us."

Caleb asked Pepi, "Do you believe in Jesus?"

"I really don't know very much about Him. I never went to a church or even a Sunday school, or read the Bible. My parents were killed when I was a little baby. I was told that they hid me under a bed when some people broke into out home. Later on, I was found by my grandmother. She raised me, but she was very poor and we didn't have much of anything. At least we lived in a small house and had a small amount of food to eat all the time.

When I was twelve years old, my grandmother got sick and passed away. I was basically all alone. One of our neighbors let me stay with them. I used to go for long walks in the forest. That's how I got kidnapped and taken to the island where the factory was. At least I had some food there. I had no where else to go anyway."

"Boy, you've been through a very hard life! I'm glad you're with us now," stated Mary Ruth.

"We are still in school, but we know that we can help you understand the Bible and have Jesus become your Lord and Savior," replied Caleb.

Pepi said, "I know that would be really wonderful! I'm looking forward to it."

They went back into the house and sat down with Thelma and Tom and talked with them for awhile.

Mary Ruth asked Pepi, "Are you tired? We have to get up early tomorrow to go to school, luckily, we'll be finished for the summer in a week. If your not tired, we can give you the Bible to read."

"I would love to start reading the Bible," Pepi said. They all went upstairs and Caleb and Mary Ruth took him to the spare bedroom.

Caleb gave him one of his T shirts to sleep in and the Bible. "We won't really see you until after school, but you can be with our grandparents. They will take good care of you."

Mary Ruth said, "Goodnight, see you tomorrow." Pepi hugged them both and thanked them so very much for getting him out of jail and letting him stay with them.

Mary Ruth said, "I believe the Lord brought you to us for a reason. Have a good night's sleep." They left and went to their rooms.

Pepi sat down on the bed and opened the Bible. He happened to open the book at Psalm 9 and read verse 9 and 10. It said, "The Lord also will be a refudge for the oppressed, a refudge in times of trouble. And they that know thy name will put their trust in thee; for thou, Lord, has not forsaken them that seek thee." He thought, Wow! I don't know exactly what these verses mean, but it sounds like the Lord will even help someone like me!

He then decided to open the Bible at different pages and read the first verse he would see. He opened the Bible at John 14 and read verse 6. It said, "Jesus saith unto him, I am the way, the truth, and the life, no man cometh unto the Father, but by me." Pepi thought, I definitely have to ask Caleb and Mary Ruth what that means. It sounds very interesting.

He opened the Bible again, this time it was 1 Thessalonians chapter 4, verse 14. "For if we believe that Jesus died and rose again, even so them also which sleep in Jesus will God bring with Him."

He then opened the middle of the Bible and was in Proverbs 4, and read verse 7. "Wisdom is the principal thing; therefore get wisdom: and with all thy getting get understanding." He thought to himself, That is truly what I need. I feel that everyone needs to read and understand these verses. I know that I will be helped a lot by Caleb and Mary Ruth.

The next morning Pepi finally woke up, he had no idea what time it was. He got out of bed and went downstairs.

Tom was outside mowing the lawn and Thelma was in the kitchen. Pepi entered the kitchen, smiled at Thelma and said, "Good morning. I'm sorry, but I have no idea what time it is," said Pepi.

Thelma smiled and said, "It's ten o'clock. Let me get you something to eat. How about a bowl of cereal, since it will be lunch time in about two hours. Do you like cheerios?"

"Sure, I love them!" replied Pepi.

Thelma put the cheerios in a bowl with some milk and sugar, gave it to Pepi, and sat down at the table with him. She said, "By the way, my husband has an extra watch and I know that he will be glad to lend it to you."

"Thank you so much, that will be great."

"At breakfast, Caleb and Mary Ruth told us why you were in that robbery when you were arrested. That is so sad. It basically is your word against theirs, that is if they ever get caught. There probably is no way to prove what they did to you."

"I know, I guess I'll be in big trouble when I go to court! Thank Heaven that Caleb and Mary Ruth found me and brought me here. I am so thankful!"

"We all will be praying for you that somehow the truth comes out and you are not put in prison."

Pepi said, "Caleb and Mary Ruth gave me a Bible to read last night. I read some pretty great verses although I really didn't know what they mean. Caleb and Mary Ruth said that they will explain the Bible to me and how to believe in Jesus Christ, our Lord and Savior. I am truly looking forward to that."

"I'm glad you will be learning from Caleb and Mary Ruth. I have a strong feeling that as they grow up, they will be helping many learn about Jesus, and how to be reborn in Him. His Father is God and only through Him can you be with God. God, Jesus and the Holy Spirit have helped us all so much. He is our everything!"

Just then, Tom came in, he smiled at Pepi and gave him a hug. "Did you have a good sleep?"

"You bet I did, It's so wonderful to be here with you and your wife. I have thought about Caleb and Mary Ruth for the past few years, ever since we were rescued from the factory in the Bahamas. I never thought that we would ever be together again. Mary Ruth said it was because of the Lord and I do believe that she is right. I feel that I am supposed to be with them. I want to learn more and more about the Bible and how to do God's will."

"That is truly wonderful! I'm sure you will be so thankful that all this happened."

Pepi said, "If it's okay, I'm going to go and start reading the new testament of the Bible. I know it will tell me things about Jesus, so I'm looking forward to it."

"Lunch will be around 12:30. We're probably going to have sandwiches so come and be with us. I'll get you the watch so you will know what time it is."

Chapter 11

Caleb and Mary Ruth were having lunch at school. Mary Ruth was telling Tammy how they got Pepi out of jail and the story that he told them about why he was arrested.

"Oh boy, if he told you the truth, we need to pray for him and help him if he does get released."

"We feel that he has come back to us for a reason and we plan to teach him about Jesus and why He is our true Lord and Savior," replied Calab."

"That's great! I'd love to help you!"

"Would you like to meet him today after school?"

"Of course I would. I'm looking forward to it."

Caleb then said, "I was thinking, we could go home and get Pepi and take him with us to the nursing home to see Len. I hope Pepi remembers Len. We are looking forward to finding out how Len is doing. We haven't seen him for a little while."

When school was over, Tammy went down to their house with them. They introduced her to Pepi and told him that they were going to the nursing home to visit Len.

"You mean the man named Len, who rescued us at the factory, with Tom and the police?' Pepi asked.

"Yes, he was hurt about five years ago. He protected Caleb and I when the roof of the theater caved in. He jumped on top of us and saved us from being hurt. Ever since that happened he has been paralyzed from the neck down."

"He and Sandy were supposed to get married, but he told her he didn't want to marry her until he became will again. She is still waiting. She loves him so much. We all continue to pray for him. He has never been able to move again, but at least he is alive. We still pray for his recovery and we know it will happen when the Lord wants it to," stated Caleb.

"Believe it or not, it has started to happen. Last time we saw him, he was able to move a little. We pray that he is doing even more now. By the way, he doesn't want Sandy to know until he recovers completely, so don't mention this to anyone. He doesn't want her to plan a wedding unless he is completely normal again," said Mary Ruth.

They went over to the nursing home. Len was sitting in his wheel chair. He was so surprised to meet Pepi again and hear what is happening to him now. They stayed with him and talked for quite awhile. He didn't say anything about his recovery.

Caleb thought, Things must have stopped getting better, he would have showed us if they had. Mary Ruth and Tammy basically had the same though. They all felt sad.

When it was time to go, they all hugged and kissed him. As they started walking toward the door, Len said, "Wait a minute, let me open the door for you."

They just looked at each other. He actually got out of the wheel chair and completely limped a few feet to the door!

The youngsters were so amazed! Caleb, Mary Ruth and Tammy, held their arms up, cried, praised and thanked the Lord with all their heart. Then Pepi also put his arms up and thanked the Lord!

They all ran over to Len, hugged and kissed him, and helped him back to his wheel chair.

Tammy said, "This is so very wonderful!" They all were so very happy!

"This must be my time to be healed in God's will! I am so very grateful and thankful to the Lord! In a little while, I'm going to surprise Sandy when she comes to see me. I don't think that it will be to much longer, the way I'm becoming stronger and stronger. I am so looking forward to it!"

Caleb said, "We still want to be in your wedding!" They all laughed and hugged Len again.

When they left, they danced and sang all the way to their house in gratefulness and love of God.

Thelma made them all something to eat. She and Tom wondered why the kids seemed so excited, but they didn't ask.

Tammy said, "Bye," to everyone and Tom drove her home.

The next morning, Caleb and Mary Ruth went to school and Tom and Thelma went grocery shopping. Pepi was sitting on the couch in the living room reading the Bible. All of a sudden, someone was knocking on the front door.

Pepi didn't know if he should answer it or not. He decided to see who it was and what they wanted. It was Ben, his wife, Gloria, and his parents.

Ben asked, "Is Thelma home?"

"No, she and Tom went to the grocery store," repied Pepi.

"I'm her brother, can we come in and wait until they return?"

Pepi didn't know what to do, but something in his mind said, It's okay. Let them come in.

"Okay, come in and have a seat in the living room." They all sat down.

"Buy the way," Ben asked, "Who are you? I know your not one of the grandchildren."

"I'm a friend of Caleb and Mary Ruth and I'm staying with them for awhile. I met them in the Bahamas a few years ago."

"Weren't they prisoners in a factory at that time?"

Pepi answered, "Yes they were, and so was I. I was one of the kids saved by Tom, Len, and the Nassau police. Thank the Lord for them. I am so grateful and thankful."

They talked for awhile, then heard a car pull into the driveway.

Tom asked Thelma, "Who's car is that?"

"I have no idea! Let's go in the house and find out."

They opened the front door and entered the house. They saw two old people and a lady sitting on the couch and Pepi on the chair. They just looked at each other.

All of a sudden, Ben ran out of the kitchen and hugged and kissed Thelma. Tom was ready shocked that Ben did that, when suddenly he said, "It's true Thelma! I am your twin brother!"

"What?" She though that she was hearing things!

"It's true! When is your birthday?"

"September 5th, 1902."

Ben cried, "100% true!"

Thelma started to faint! Ben and Tom picked her up and helped her to a chair. Thelma was crying in joy and happiness!

Ben smiled and said, "This is my step parents, Dr. Ken and Lynn Davidson. The people who were taking care of us while our real parents were taking a walk with their pet tigers. That is when the pirates came to the island. They carried us unto the pirate ship and saved us from being left on the island."

Thelma was just staring at Ben's parents. All of a sudden, she ran over and hugged and kissed them. She said, "Thank you so much for taking care of us!"

They were crying too, they were so happy that Thelma was alive and that they got to see her again.

Thelma then asked, "Why did we not know each other for all these years?"

"It's a pretty long story and if you want, we can talk about it now," replied Ben.

"I truly want to hear it!" Thelma jumped up and hugged Ben again. They all thanked God for getting them together.

They all sat down and Ben and his step parents told the whole story to her and Tom. Pepi also listened. Thelma was totally in shock when she heard what happened.

She again went over to Ben's step parents and said, "Thank you so very much for all the things you did for us. I love you both!" They all started crying again in love, happiness and praise to the Lord.

Dr. Ken said, "The Lord was truly we us! We were so upset when you were kidnapped. We thought that you were killed. It is so wonderful that you are still alive and we are all together again. We've always loved and missed you all these years."

Lynn said, "I do believe that everything happens for a reason."

Ben replied, "I can't help but to think the reason might be our three grandchildren, Tammy, Caleb, and Mary Ruth. They are so different than other children when it comes to the Lord. I do feel that they all have a great destiny with the Lord." They all said, "Amen."

Thelma sat back down and said, "I can't believe I had been on an island and my parents had been stranded there by themselves after we were taken away. It must have been a real calamity when Ben and

I were kidnapped. At least you got Ben back. I wonder what happened to me? All I remember is living in an orphanage and being adopted. Unfortunatelly, both my step parents have died, so if they did know anything, I can never find out. Can I please make you all lunch and you can meet my grandchildren, Caleb and Mary Ruth, when they get home from school.?"

Doctor Ken said, "We would certainly love to meet them!"

Please, sister in law, let me help you with lunch!" said Gloria. Thelma and Gloria hugged each other and went out to the kitchen.

"What do you think of Thelma?" Ben asked his step parents.

Lynn replied, "She is a sweet, beautiful lady and she was a sweet beautiful baby. We are so thankful that she is alive, doing well, has a great husband and grandchildren." She smiled and winked at Tom.

Doctor Ken asked, "Ben, can we please praise the Lord and thank Him again?"

Ben said, "Let's hold hands and praise the Lord."

"DEAR LORD, WE ARE SO THANKFUL TO YOU FOR BRINGING ME AND MY TWIN SISTER, THELMA, TOGETHER. WE HAVEN'T SEEN EACH OTHER FOR 69 YEARS, OR KNOWN THAT WE EACH EXISTED. THANK YOU THAT WE ARE BOTH ALIVE AND DOING WELL IN OUR LIVES. WE KNOW THAT YOU HAVE ALWAYS BEEN WITH US, LEADED, AND GUIDED US TO BE GRATEFUL AND THANKFUL SO VERY MUCH FOR OUR LIVES AND OUR WONDERFUL GRANDCHILDREN, WHO YOU HAVE ALSO LED AND PROTECTED ALL THEIR LIVES. I KNOW THAT THEY WILL DO YOUR WILL. THANK YOU ALSO THAT DOCTOR KEN AND LYNN, WHO SAVED US, THROUGH YOU, AND RAISED ME, ARE HERE WITH US. DEAR LORD, YOU ARE SO WONDERFUL! YOU ARE OUR EVERYTHING AND WE WILL ALWAYS HAVE FAITH IN YOU. THANK YOU AGAIN FOR ALL YOUR LOVE AND GOODNESS! IN JESUS HOLY NAME, AMEN."

At school, Caleb and Mary Ruth were talking to Tammy at lunch time. Tammy said, "Guess what! My great grandparents came down from PA. to see us. They are such great people. They are in their 90's!"

"Wow, you have great grandparents!" said Mary Ruth. "Thank God we have our grandparents. The sad thing is that we don't have our wonderful parents. We miss them so much! They are up in Heaven with the Lord."

"Our dad was also a pastor like your grandfather. He was so wonderful! Everyone in the church loved him and his sermons were so great. He mainly spoke about our Lord Jesus Christ. Our church was in Davie, next to Ft. Lauderdale. It was amazing. Every week, more and more people would come including children. Dad was even thinking that he soon would be needing a bigger church." replied Cable.

"My mom was also a wonderful person and the people loved her. She was so kind to everyone. She would help them in any way she could. We miss them so much!" cried Mary Ruth.

"We learned so much about our Lord and Savior, Jesus Christ, from both of them when we were children. Then in 1966, our house burned down. Luckily we were able to escape but my mom and dad were already dead. Someone slit both their throats. We had no idea who would have done such a thing. We hid in the barn and we did see two men outside. Suddenly, a voice, in my head told me that we should run and hide. I know that it was God who said that to me. From that point on, we have been through a lot, but the Lord took care of us and still does. We are so thankful to Him! Nothing to bad has happened to us for awhile, thank the Lord, things seem to be going fine." Caleb said.

Tammy cried, "My goodness, I have to tell you that some similar things happened to me in my life. Thank God that I still have my parents, but they were worried about me for quite awhile. I do know that mainly because of my grandfather, I learned how to have complete faith that the Lord would take care of me and He truly did.

"We have to go back to class in a few minutes, but can you tell us your story sometime?" asked Mary Ruth.

"Of course, I'll be more than glad to. It happened five years ago in 1966."

Caleb and Mary Ruth looked at each other. Mary Ruth said, "Believe it or not, that's when things started happening to us!"

"Your kidding," cried Tammy. "Maybe we can get together one night and I'll you my whole story of 1966."

"That would be great! We also were through a lot more than we have told you. This is very interesting that we all went through a lot of problems in 1966, now we are together, and are such great friends. I do believe there is a special reason for this," stated Caleb.

"How about you come over to our house tomorrow night and we can discuss everything. Pepi can also listen to our conversation. I think it might help him to understand our faith in the Lord.. It should help him believe in God's Son, our Lord and Savior, Jesus Christ, when he hears how he has taken care of us, because of our true faith in him. I do believe that the three of us have a destiny to do the Lord's will now and in the future."

"That would be so wonderful if we can be together, do God's will, and help others to become strong, faithful, loving Christains. Talk to you both tomorrow night." They all went back to class.

Chapter 12

After school, Caleb and Mary Ruth stopped and visited Len. He was still doing great, even better than the last time they were with him. They were so very happy. Then they went home. As they walked toward the house, they saw a car in the diveway.

"I wonder who's here? I've never seen that car before," said Mary Ruth.

"Well, we'll soon find out!"

They entered the front door and saw a group of people sitting in the living room. They recognized Pastor Ben and his wife, but had no idea who the older people were.

Thelma jumped up and ran over to them. Tears were rolling down her face.

"What's wrong?" asked Caleb.

"Nothing is wrong! I'm crying in happiness! She took them over to Pastor Ben.

"Kids, I'd like you to meet my twin brother, Pastor Ben, who is your great uncle!"

Caleb and Mary Ruth were shocked. Ben jumped up, hugged and kissed them.

"I'm so glad to meet my great niece and nephew! Now I want you to meet my step parents, Doctor Ken and Lynn Davidson. They saved my life and your grandmother's when we were babies."

Caleb and Mary Ruth hugged Ken and Lynn. They were astounded!

Caleb asked, "Were you the doctor on the island that gave birth to the twins?"

"You are the people we read about in the journal?" asked Mary Ruth.

"Granny, you and Pastor Ben were the twins and Doctor Ken and Lynn saved you!" asked Caleb.

Mary Ruth cried, "Granny, you mean that it was your parents bones we found in the cave and buried on the island?"

"Yes, your questions are absolutely right, in fact, those bones you found were your real great grandparents!" Thelma replied.

Caleb and Mary Ruth could hardly believe their ears.

Pastor Ben said, "The tigers you saw were related to your great grandparents pet tigers."

Caleb and Mary Ruth just stared at each other, they were so stunned. Caleb said, "We had no idea when we read the journal that the things you just told us could be!"

"That means that we're part Scottish!" Mary Ruth smiled and said. They all grinned.

Caleb said to Doctor Ken and Lynn, "We are so very grateful and thankful to you for saving our grandmother and great uncle." He and Mary Ruth jumped up and hugged and kissed them again. "Your also Tammy's great grandparents!"

Pastor Ben said, "I believe the Lord led them to help us."

'God has taken such great care of all of us!" Mary Ruth cried.

Caleb cried, "Let us pray to the Lord!"

"DEAR LORD, THANK YOU EVER SO MUCH FOR BEING WITH US AND ALWAYS HELPING US. WE ALL TRULY LOVE YOU AND HAVE COMPLETE FAITH IN YOU. YOU ARE OUR GOD, OUR FATHER, OUR LORD, OUR HOLY SPIRIT, OUR REDEEMER, OUR CREATOR, OUR SHEPARD, OUR ROCK, OUR SALVATION, OUR COUNSEL, OUR GUIDANCE, OUR LEADER, OUR FRIEND, OUR WISDOM, OUR KNOWLEDGE, OUR STRENGTH, OUR JOY, OUR HOPE, OUR LOVE, OUR LIFE, OUR UNDERSTANDING, OUR HELPER, OUR TEACHER, OUR MENTOR, OUR COMPANION, OUR EVERYTHING!

WE WORSHIP YOU, WE PRAISE YOU, WE ADORE YOU, WE ADMIRE YOU, WE HONOR YOU, WE RESPECT YOU, WE

LOVE YOU, WE NEED YOU, WE WANT YOU, WE CHERISH YOU, WE THANK YOU.

WITHOUT YOU, WE ARE NOTHING. PLEASE CONTINUE TO BE WITH US, HELP US, LEAD US, AND GUIDE US TO DO YOUR WILL. WE TRULY THANK YOU FOR EVERYTHING! IN JESUS HOLY NAME, AMEN."

Pastor Ben said to Caleb, "That was an assume prayer. I know that you, Mary Ruth, and Tammy have a great future with the Lord!" They all said, "Thank you!"

Doctor Ken and his wife both smiled and he said, "I am so very glad that we got to meet you, Thelma, and your wonderful grandchildren! We never in a million years thought that this would happen. We know it happened because of our wonderful Lord!"

Ben said, "We have to go home now. I know it was such an exciting day for all of us and I am sure my step parents need a rest."

"We would like to invite you all over for lunch on Sunday after church," Gloria said."

"We all would love to join you in church and hear my wonderful brother in law's sermon, and of course have lunch!" replied Tom.

They all stood up, hugged each other and said, "See you in church!"

Ben, Gloria, Doctor Ken and Lynn got in their car and left for their home in Kissimmee.

Thelma was so happy, she hugged Tom and the kids again! "Wow, what a wonderful day this has been! I knew Ben for awhile now and something came to me the day I met him! I knew he had my twin brother's name but I never, ever, thought that he really was my twin brother!"

Tom replied, "The more I look at both of you when you are together, there is a likeness in your face, especially your blue eyes!"

"Caleb and I are also so happy that Pastor Ben is your twin brother, and we are so glad to meet the people who saved you both!"

"I was shocked to find out that the bones we found were our great grandparents! I wonder what exactly happened to them?" asked Caleb.

"Well," said Thelma, perhaps we'll never know, but I love them and I truly miss them. I don't even remember anything about them. I was a very young baby when all this happened. I don't even know what they look like. I'm going to go now and start supper. I bet that we're all pretty hungry!"

"I'll help you. I am hungry!" Tom replied.

Caleb and Mary Ruth sat down with Pepi. He was really surprised about all the things that happened today. He said, "I truly want to believe in the Lord and have complete love and faith in Him!"

"We know that we have a great destiny to fulfill and it is the number one thing for us." Caleb said. "If you would like to be with us, we'll be glead to have you, but you must truly believe in Jesus. I'm sure that Tammy will be with us, she is very much like us in her believes, love, and faith. We will all help you and teach you from now on."

"I am so hopeful and excited to walk in God's narrow path of righteousness with you."

"Now I know for sure that you have been reading the Bible!" Mary Ruth replied.

"I sure have been, but I need a lot of study to understand it completely."

"Don't worry, you will learn and understand every thing that Mary Ruth, Tammy, Pastor Ben, and I teach you."

Pepi replied, "The only thing that I'm worried about is if I'm going to be put in jail."

Caleb said, "Start having faith in the Lord that you will be with us, not in jail."

"Your truly right. Please pray for me."

"We already have been. We love you and want you with us," Mary Ruth said.

"Right now, Mary Ruth and I are going to start doing our homework. Do you want to watch television?"

"No thanks, I'll be reading the Bible." Caleb and Mary Ruth hugged him, sat down with him, and did their homework.

Mary Ruth said, "In a week, we won't have any more homework. School will be over for the summer."

Forty five minutes later, supper was ready. It was so good. "Granny is such a great cook!"

Chapter 13

The next day, after school, Tammy came over to their house. Pepi went out on the back porch with them and sat down. Tammy started telling them what she had been through in 1966.

Tammy said, "I was only seven years old and in second grade back then. One day I was walking home from school, there was only a week more until the summer vacation. My friend, Debbie, who I walked home with everyday, wasn't with me, she wasn't feeling good so she stayed home from school that day.

As I was walking, a black car pulled up aside of me. The man asked me if I knew where Indiana avenue was located.

I told him that I was sorry, I didn't know how to get there from where I was walking. All of a sudden, the man jumped out of the car, grabbed me, and put something over my nose and mouth. I became unconscious.

When I woke up, I was laying on a bed in a bedroom. I had no idea where I was and started crying. I didn't know what I should do. I thought, I have to get out of this house, but I have no idea where I am. I got out of the bed and looked out of the window.

I knew I wasn't in the town of St. Cloud. I saw many cows eating grass. I also saw what looked like a big lake. In a distance, I could see a bunch of houses that were close together.

What am I going to do? I thought to myself. Suddenly, the bedroom door opened. The same man who was driving the car came in with a bowl of soup and a glass of water.

He said, Here is your supper. You have ten minutes to eat it, then he left the room. I was hungry and very thirsty. I drank some water, then started eating the soup.

I later was told that around this time, my mother was wondering where I was. She was thinking, Did she stop at one of her friends houses? If she did, she should have called me and left me know. I was three hours late at that time. My mom called my dad, who was at work, and told him what was happening. He told her to please call all her friends and ask if Tammy was there. He told her that he would be leaving work in a little while and that he would drive around all the streets and look to see if I had fallen down and hurt myself and couldn't walk.

My mom then called all my friends, hoping that I would be there, but I wasn't. My mom, Carol, was so upset. Just then, my brother, Derrick, got home and she told him what was going on. They hugged each other, they were so very upset. Mom then called the police and told them what happened.

They told her that they were not allowed to do anything until a child is missing for twenty four hours, but the officer said, Believe me, we will keep our eyes open for her.

My dad got home and told them that he had not seen me. They then called my grandfather, Pastor Ben. He and Gloria came right over. They all prayed for me, that I was all right and I would be found.

In the mean time, the man came back and picked up the glass and the soup bowl. He asked me if I had to go to the bathroom, which I truly did. He took me to it and waited outside the door, when I was finished, he took me back and locked me in the bedroom.

A few hours later, I got in the bed and fell asleep. I had been crying because I was so scared. As I was sleeping, the man came in the room. He laid down beside me. I woke up because he was rubbing his hands up and down my body, even on my chest. He turned me over and continued to rub his hands all over me. Suddenly, he got on top of me and started pulling my clothes off. I was totally in shock and crying. I had no idea what he was trying to do. Just then, he heard the phone outside of the bedroom start ringing.

He then said to me, I'll be right back! I have to answer the phone. It probably is my boss wanting to tell me what to do with you. He went out and locked the door. I didn't know what to do but something told me to get up and go to the window.

Something then told me to pick up the lamp, smash the window, jump out, and run as fast as I can. That's just what I did! I smashed the window, jumped out, and ran into the woods.

A few minutes later, I heard the man start yelling and cursing. Apparently, he saw the smashed window and came out to find me. It was dark, but I saw a tree that had fallen on the ground with a deep space underneath it. I jumped under it and covered myself with leaves. Then I heard the man walking by and saying some bad words. Luckily, he didn't find me and I heard him start walking back to the house.

Again, I heard a voice say to me, Getup, run, and keep on running. That's what I did. I was so tired and in shock. It was really a wonder that I was able to do what I did. I now am sure the Lord was helping me.

Next thing, I had come to a road. I didn't know which way to go or what to do. A car came around the corner and of course I was really scared, since that crazy man put me in his car. I thought, It's probably him! I started crying more.

The car came up to me and stopped. A man got out and came over to me. I was hysterical by then. He hugged me and said, It's okay, honey, I'm a police officer. We were told to watch out for a little lost girl and to bring her down to the police station if we found her. What's your name?

I said Tammy Lee Wylie. He said, you are the one! Come on honey, we'll get you back with your parents. He then put me in his police car. I heard him radio the police station and tell them that he found me on a road in the country. They told him that they will notify my parents. I don't even remember what that officer looked like or his name.

My parents and grandparents were so happy and thankful to God that I was found. They told me later that they got down on their knees, praised and thanked God, then drove down to the police station.

When I arrived, my parents and grandparents ran over, hugged me and kissed me with tears running down their faces. I was still in complete shock about what almost happened to me. I didn't say a word. The police asked me what happened but I didn't want to think or talk about it.

My family took me home. They were so happy, but I was hardly moving or talking. They knew I was acting strangely and wondered what I had been through."

Caleb looked at her and said, "Your story is very interesting, as to the fact that we did some of the same things, such as break a window with a lamp. hide under a fallen tree, and kept walking until we came to a road. What happened then was how we got to St. Cloud and I'm sure that it was God's will. That's how he saved you also! I am amazed!"

"We're so sorry to hear what you have been through, but thank the Lord that He saved you and you weren't raped by that man who kidnapped you," said Mary Ruth.

"The problem with me was, at that time I knew God and Jesus, but I didn't really know a lot. Especially that the Lord would help me and save me by having true faith in Him. I was so very thankful that I was saved, but at that time I didn't realize that it was God who saved me.

After I went home, I was still in shock for weeks. My parents tried to help me understand about God, but my mind was in another place. I just couldn't comprehend what they were saying to me. Something strange was happening in my mind. I now believe that it was Satan doing it.

A few days after they were trying to help me, my parents told my grandpa, Pastor Ben and my grandma what really was going on with me. From that point on, he came over and spent time with me everyday. He prayed and prayed for me, along with my parents and grandma. He prayed to the Lord, that if Satan was in me, to please make him leave.

As he would be praying for me, I would be jumping up and down, holding my ears, screaming and crying.

Finally, in about three weeks I completely changed. I stopped jumping, then I stopped holding my ears, and finally I stopped screaming and crying.

Suddenly, I just looked at them, smiled, ran over and hugged and kissed them all! They knew that the Lord had preformed a miricle on me and brought me back to them.

My grandpa explained what had happened in me. I said to my grandpa, I truly thank God for helping me become normal again. Please teach me everything in the Bible so I will understand the work of God and His Son, Jesus Christ!

Grandpa smiled at me, and said, You bet I will! I truly want to do that for you. Before, you never wanted to learn anything. I'm sure that this is one of my destinies in life.

From that day on, I have been learning and understanding, more and more of God's word and how we must truly repent of our sins and make Jesus Christ our Lord and Savior. I'm also so glad that you both are with me and I pray that Pepi will be with us. Now he can join us in our Bible studies with my grandpa and we can also teach him."

Mary Ruth said, "I feel that the reason we met you and became such good friends was because we must learn more from the Bible so we can bring others to Jesus."

"I agree, I give my entire life to God and His Son, our Lord and Savior," replied Tammy.

Caleb asked Pepi, "What do you think about all this?"

"What Tammy said is also truly amazing! I truly believe what she said, how God helped her and took care of her, like he does for you and Mary Ruth. I am giving myself also to Him because now I realize how many times He has saved me and healed me. I had no idea that He was with me!

I know that I have a lot to learn, but I also know how the three of you and your grandpa will help me. I just pray that I will not get put into jail. I want to be with you and someday be able to teach people."

Tammy said, "We also want you to be with us. We pray to the Lord that it will happen." She looked at her watch and said, "Well, I better go home. It was so very great having this talk together. I feel so strong in the Lord!"

"We do too, We do too!" cried Mary Ruth. "See you at school tomorrow."

Chapter 14

Tammy started to go out of the house and was planing to walk home by herself.

Caleb asked, "Would you like me to walk over to your house with you? I know you only live a few blocks away, but it is starting to get dark."

"That will be fine! Let's go."

They left and started walking to Tammy's house. They only went five blocks and it was dark.

Caleb said, "I'm glad that I came with you."

In the next block, they walked past a bar room. As they passed it, the door opened and three drunk men came out. When they saw Tammy, they started walking toward her.

Caleb said to Tammy, "Those men are heading toward us.." He turned around and looked at them and said, "Our Lord and Savior is with us, leave us alone!"

The men stopped and suddenly ran away. Tammy said, "Thank you, Caleb, I can't help to think that when you mentioned our Lord to them, they knew that he would protect us and that's why they ran away."

"I don't know if that's why they ran, but it might be true."

When they got to Tammy's house, Caleb hugged her and said, "See you tomarrow."

"Wait, I'm going to ask my dad to drive you home. You don't need to run into those drunken guys again." Tammy's dad drove Caleb home.

When he got home, he told Mary Ruth what happened. Mary Ruth said, "Oh boy, I'm so glad that we are so strong in the Lord. I know He wants us to do His will and meet our destiny." They went to their rooms to say their prayers and then went to sleep.

The next day at school, the kids were all taking end of the year tests in all subjects. Only two more days and they would be on their summer vacation. Again, they were having lunch with all of their friends who attended their Bible studies and Tammy, their helper.

Caleb suggested, "Since we're going to be out of school for the summer, I think that we should have our Bible study two days a week instead of one. If anyone goes away on a vacation, one of us can take them aside and teach them the Bible studies that they missed while they were away. Meanwhile, we're going to have to do a lot of extra teaching for Pepi if he is able to be here."

That evening, Paul called them and told them that Pepi's trial will be at 10AM on Monday morning and said he would take him there.

"We'll be done school on Friday, can we go with you on Monday?" asked Caleb.

"Sure, I'll pick you all up at 8:30 to make sure that we're not late."

When Caleb hung up the phone, he told Pepi, Mary Ruth, and his grandparents that Pepi's trail will be this coming Monday.

They all hugged Pepi and told him that they would pray that he wouldn't get put in jail, but if he did, it would happen for a reason.

On Monday, they arrived in Orlando and entered the court room. Pepi had been put with his lawyer that was given to him.

When the trial started, Pepi was put on a chair next to the judge and had to swear to tell the whole truth and nothing but the truth so help you God, which he promised. He was then questioned by the prosecuting lawyer.

Pepi did tell the truth as to what happened and why, in the robbery, but there was no possible why that he could prove any of it. There was also no way his lawyer could convince anyone that he was telling the truth.

The judge then ordered him to ten years in prison for the robbery he committed.

Caleb, Mary Ruth and Paul were stunned! Pepi was crying and taken to a jail cell at the police station and then would be driven to the prison in Wildwood.

Paul, Caleb, and Mary Ruth went to see him in the jail cell. He was still crying. Pepi cried, "I should have left them shoot me instead of helping them in a robbery!"

"Pepi, continue to have faith in the Lord. I know that he will help you!" cried Mary Ruth.

Caleb said, "Yes, trust in God!"

"Pepi, do not give up. Be brave and strong. The Lord is your strength and shield. You must trust Him and He will help you. Pour out your feelings to the Lord, as you would pour water out of a jug. If your heart is broken, you'll find God right there. If you were kicked in your gut, He will help you catch your breath," said Paul.

Mary Ruth then opened her purse and handed Pepi a small Bible. "Please continue to read this and keep your faith."

Pepi took the Bible from her and said, "I promise that I will." They then had to leave.

Caleb said, "We will never stop praying for Pepi. He has repented of his sins and believes in Jesus Christ. He has come to God through Him."

As they were driving home, Paul said, "I'm so sorry that this happened to Pepi, but there was no way that he could prove his innocence."

"We understand why they put him in prison. It surly appears that he was one of the robbers and the judge probably thinks he was lying so he would not be found guilty," stated Caleb.

When they got home, they told everyone what happened. They all were so sad and said that they would pray for him.

Pepi was taken to the prison and put in a cell with a very nasty man. When he was reading the Bible, the man would start saying nasty things to him and yelling. The only time Pepi could read the Bible and understand some of it, was when his cell mate was sleeping. It was so sad being in prison.

Pepi thought, I wanted to be with Caleb and Mary Ruth so much and learn more about Jesus. Now here I am in a cell with a nasty man and not helping the Lord.

Two weeks later, Pepi was very sick in his stomach. He was taken to a nurse to be checked. They gave him some medicine and sent him back to his cell. As he was about to enter, he saw that his cell mate, Raymond Hopkins, was reading something. When he entered, Raymond looked at him, threw the book on the floor, and rolled over on his bed.

Pepi looked on the floor and picked his Bible up. He said, Ray, don't worry, I will let you read my Bible."

"I don't want to read it," Ray shouted.

"Then why were you reading it?"

"I wasn't reading it! I can't! I need glasses to read and I don't have any!"

Pepi asked, "How about I read it to you and you can learn some things about Jesus?"

Ray turned around and said, "I don't believe in Jesus! But I don't have anything else to do, so I might listen, unless I fall asleep."

Pepi said, "Okay, I'll start reading now. I'm going to start reading the New Testiment, which is all about Jesus, Our Lord and Savior."

Pepi read for an hour. He didn't know if Ray was listing or sleeping because he was turned over on his bed.

In a little while they were taken to the lunchroom to eat. Pepi didn't say anything about the Bible. As they were finishing their lunch, Ray asked, "When are you going to read again?"

Pepi thought, Oh thank you Lord! He must have been listening and liked what he heard. He said, "I can start again as soon as we go back to our cell."

"Okay, I might listen or I might not, it's up to you if you want to read out loud."

Pepi read again out loud. Again Ray was laying against him. Pepi still didn't know for sure if he was listening, but something made him feel that he was.

From that point on, Pepi read at least five hours a day. After a week, Ray had tuned toward him. Pepi felt that it was bringing him to the Lord.

A few days later, Ray said to Pepi, "I do now believe in the Lord, Jesus Christ and that He is our Savior! I pray that he will forgive me for all the sins I have done in my life! I never heard the Bible before, but Pepi, I'm so thankful that you have read it to me. I feel like my life will be changing, as I want to be with the Lord now and help others. The Bible has helped me to understand, without a doubt, that Jesus has died on the cross so our sins will be forgiven and that we can come to God, his Father, through him. I wish I would have known about Jesus long ago, I'm sure I would never have been the nasty person I am, but will never be from now on!"

Pepi went over to him and shook his hand. Ray stood up, hugged him, and said, "Please continue to read to me."

"Of course I will! I know that the Lord has forgiven you of your sins by confessing. You are reborned in Jesus, our Lord and Savior, as I was."

They begain talking more and becoming good friends. Other prisoners were surprised to see the change in Ray. He used to be a very mean and nasty person. Now he would smile and great others. The officers were also stunned to see the change in him.

Pepi was in prison nearly a month and a half now. As he prayed to God, he thanked him that he was able to bring Ray to the Lord and basically change his life.

Caleb, Mary Ruth, and Tammy had visted him a couple of times with Paul and Pepi told them what was happening. They were really happy to hear it. Now they truly believed that some day Pepi would be with them.

About a week later, an officer came to Pepi's cell and took him to the warden's office. Pepi had no idea why he was there. The warden smiled at him and said, "I heard from our officers that you read the Bible out loud a lot and it really changed your cell mate, Ray. That is truly wonderful because he was a really bad man. I don't think that very many prisoners here believe in Jesus Christ, but now at least one of the worst men completely does."

"Thank you. I fell like I was truly doing God's will and I was learning too!"

"We truly thank you for what you did. Actually, that's not the reason we brought you up here, although we love what you did."

Pepi stared at him and asked, "What is the reason I'm here?"

"On Wednesday, you are going back to court in Orlando."

"What does that mean?" Pepi asked.

"The reason is, they finally caught the two men that were in the robbery with you. They were caught robbing a grocery store and were also identified by the man who was working at the gas station in the robbery you were in. The two men were questioned about the robbery at the gas station, they finally admitted to it and that they made you be with them by threating to kill you if you didn't do what they told you."

Pepi nearly fell off the chair when he heard this. He folded his hands, held them up, and said, "Thank you my Dear Lord! I had complete faith in You, that someday, something great would happen to me! Thank You so much! I give my life to you forever and promise to do Your will."

The warden walked over and hugged Pepi and said, "I also thank the Lord. I believe you are a wonderful person and will do His will."

Pepi asked, " Would you please call a St. Cloud police officer named Paul Legna and let him know when my court apparence will be?"

"I'll be more than happy to. Meanwhile, you can go back to your cell and read the Bible to Ray."

When Pepi got back to his cell, he told Ray what happened. Ray said, "Thank You Dear Lord! I will be very sad that you are leaving me and I will miss you. I love you and truly thank you for bringing me to the Lord!"

"I will give my Bible to you," said Pepi.

"Thank you, I truly appreciate it, but how am I going to read it?"

"Somehow, someway, sometime, I know you will be able to read it. Now I will continue reading to you while I'm with you."

Holy Bible

Chapter 15

Monday finally arrived. Pepi hugged Ray and Ray said, "Good luck, I know you will be following God's plan for you."

"I will also keep praying for you," replied Pepi.

The officer came to the cell and took him to the police car and they headed for Orlando. When he came out in the court room with his lawyer, he saw Caleb, Mary Ruth, Tammy, and Paul sitting in the attendants seats. They all smiled at him and folded their hands.

His lawyer stood up and told the judge everything about the real robbers admitting that Pepi was only with them because they threatened to kill him if he didn't help them in the robbery of a gas station.

After he finished, the judge asked the persecuting attorney how he felt. The attorney said, "We are so sorry that we didn't believe Pepi when he confessed that, but there was no proof that he was telling the truth, now there is. We want to release Pepi from his sentence."

"The judge smiled and said, "I agree, Pepi, you are free to go!" Pepi and all his friends were crying in happiness and thankfulness to the Lord. They all ran over and hugged Pepi.

Tammy said, "We knew that this day would come and we are so very thankful that it happened!" They all got in Thelma's car that Paul was driving and praised the Lord and thanked Him again.

As they were driving back to St. Cloud, Pepi told them about his cell mate, Ray, and how he completely changed.

"That is so wonderful that a nasty man like that would completely change in such a short time with your help," said Caleb.

"It was amazing, but there is one problem now. I always read the Bible to him because he can't see the words good enough to read it himself. I gave the Bible to him, but I don't know how he's going to be able to read it."

They arrived at Caleb and Mary Ruth's home. When they entered, besides seeing Thelma and Tom, there was Jane, Josh, Sandy, and Len was in his wheelchair.

They all clapped when Pepi entered the room, hugged and kissed him. Thelma said, "We all felt that this was going to happen! I hope you all are hungry, Jane, Sandy, and I made a great meal!"

They all filled their plates with whatever they wanted and sat down and talked about all that Pepi had been through and did with his cell mate.

Mary Ruth said, "His cellmate, Ray, is unable to read the Bible because he can't see."

"Maybe he just needs some reading glasses," Sandy replied.

Josh said, "I have an extra pair he can have." Then Tom said, "So do I."

Pepi exclaimed, "Wow, if that's all he needs, that will be wonderful!"

"If you want, tomorrow when I'm finished working, we can all ride up there again, go to the warden, and ask him if Ray can have the glasses," said Paul.

"That will be great!" cried Pepi,

When they finished eating, they all prayed together and thanked God for helping Pepi and Ray.

Sandy was sitting aside of Len in his wheelchair. She looked at him, smiled and said, "I'm so sorry that your still unable to move. We all have been praying for you for a long time and we will keep on praying forever. We know it will happen if it is supposed to. I will also wait for you forever. You are the man I love and always will be."

Len smiled at her and said, "Thank you for your love. I also love you and told you that we wouldn't get married until I recover. You have waited so long and kept on loving me. I thank you so much." He then put his hand on her. She was amazed and shouded, "Oh Dear God!"

Everybody looked over at her and Len. All of a sudden, Len stood up and pushed the wheelchair away! He then got down on his knees and said, "Sandy, will you marry me?"

This time Sandy did faint! Len shook her and said, "Wake up Sandy!" She opened her eyes, sat up, and hugged him.

Again, everyone was crying in happiness and thanking the Lord!

Sandy said, ""Len, I am so very happy! How did this happen?"

Len told them all the story of how God sent a great doctor to him and that he was the only one, out of many, that healed in the last year. He also said, "The kids knew what was going on with me for awhile, but I told them not to say anything about what was happening to me. They truly listened to me. I still am not 100% healed, but I know now that I will be. The Lord is with me and I will do his will. I can't wait until we get married!"

Everyone was ao happy and thankful. Jane said, "What a wonderful Lord we have! If only everyone would realize that they should be reborned in Jesus and have faith, love, trust, and hope in Him and God His Father. He will help them when the time is right. We all have been through a lot, but here we are, all together and doing fine."

The next afternoon, Paul took Caleb, Mary Ruth, Tammy, and Pepi up to the prison. They were taken in to see the warden. Pepi did the talking, he said, "Sir, you know that I have been released and that I am so thankful. My plan now is to be with Caleb, Mary Ruth and Tammy and do God's will. I have a lot to learn, but someday I will be with them teaching others about our Lord, Jesus Christ, and how He was crucified on the cross so that out sins would be forgiven and we can be with God, His Father, through him."

The warden smiled and said, "It is so wonderful what you are planning!"

Pepi then showed him the two pairs of glasses, told him about Ray's problem, and that the glasses might help him to be able to read the Bible.

"That would be great if the glasses can help him. I promise that I will give them to him." They all talked for a little while, then left and Paul drove them home.

As they were getting out of the car, Caleb said, "Paul, we thank you so much for all the things you do to help us in so many ways."

Paul said, "I will always help you all, you can depend on me. By the way Caleb, would you like me to teach you how to drive? You are sixteen and soon will be seventeen, so you are the right age."

"That would be really great, I'd love to get a drivers license! Pepi, do you have a license?"

"No, I sure don't. I never had anyone who would teach me. I either walk or take a bus."

"That's fine, I'll teach both of you!" replied Paul. "See you soon. I'll give you a call when we can start."

"Great, we're looking forward to it." They all hugged him and said goodbye.

Sandy was at Len's room at the nusing home. She said, "Len, I am so happy and thankful that you are nearly completely recovered!! I thank the Lord with all my heart! Do you still want us to get married?"

Len smiled, hugged her and said, "You know I do! I don't know how much longer I have to stay here and have my treatments. Now I don't have anywhere to live, since I wasn't able to pay for my house, I lost it. It was sold several years ago at an auction. Thank God that the police department kept my insurance for me."

"Of course you can stay at my mom and dad's house. You know we do have a spare room since Caleb and Mary Ruth moved in with their grandmother."

"Thank you so much, that will be great! I'm pretty sure that Captain Hardy will give me a job again if there is one available."

"Can I tell Captain Hardy how you doing now?"

"Sure, I know he will be shocked, he always comes to see me at least once a week and I never showed him that I was able to move because I didn't want anyone to know before I surprised you. Caleb, Mary Ruth, and Tammy had known but I knew that I could depend on them not to say anything."

"Well, that was the best surprise I ever had! cried Sandy. "Did you know that I was going to faint?"

"Of course not! It scared me for a second, but you came back quickly. Once I get my job back and we get married, we should be able to afford to buy a house. I can't wait! Of course we can have a bunch of kids also!"

Sandy smiled, hugged and kissed him. "I better get going. I have to go to work tomorrow. I'll see you tomorrow when work is over. I love you. Bye."

At the prison, the warden walked down to Ray's cell with some prison guards. Ray was sitting on his bed with his eyes closed.

One of the guards yelled, "Ray, wake up, the warden is here to see you."

Ray opened his eyes and saw the warden standing outside the cell. He walked over and said, "Hello sir."

The warden asked him how he was feeling. "I'm doing fine, but I sure do miss my x cellmate, Pepi. We weren't together all that long, but he completely changed my life. Now I just sit here and and think about what I learned, but I would like to learn more."

The warden said, "I heard that you now have a Bible."

"I do, but there's no way I can read it, my eyes are bad."

The warden smiled and said, "Maybe these will help you." He handed him two pairs of glasses.

Ray was stunned! "Thank you so much! I pray they work! Where did they come from and how did you ever know that I needed them?"

"Your x cellmate, Pepi, and his friends came here yesterday and brought them to me. Pepi explained your problem and we all hope that these will help you."

Ray put one of the glasses on, got the Bible, and opened it. He said, "Oh no, I can see the words a little, but there's no way I can read them. He then put the other pair on and looked again at the Bible. Thank You, my wonderful Lord! I can see the words really good! Now I will be able to read it!"

"We wish you good luck, we are aware that the short time you had with Pepi changed you. I hope that you can become even better now."

"I know the Lord will somehow help me to understand the Bible. He truly has already!"

Ray was so happy that Pepi and his friends had brought him the glasses. He sat down and started reading.

The warden called Paul at the St. Cloud police station and told him that one pair of the glasses helped Ray tremendously.

Paul said, "I'm so glad to hear that and so will Pepi and his friends. Thank you for letting me know."

That night after work, he went over to Thelma's house and told Caleb, Pepi, and Mary Ruth the good news. They were all thrilled!

"As we teach Pepi and our friends, we'll take notes about what the verses mean and send them to Ray," replied Caleb. "That way he will truly understand the meaning of the Bible. Of course, we always talk with my great uncle, Pastor Ben, before we teach. Sometimes, he even comes over and teaches with us. He is so smart! I'm so glad that we found out that he is our great uncle."

As Paul was ready to leave, Sandy came in the door. She smiled and said, "Hi," to everybody. "I just wanted to let you all know that in two weeks, Len will be leaving the nursing home and moving in my parents house. He will then have to go to the treatment center three times a week for awhile and when he is finished, he can try to get his job as a police officer back again. Then we will start planing our wedding! Caleb and Mary Ruth will be in it, of course!"

Caleb and Mary Ruth hugged her and said, "We can't wait!"

"Neither can I and I thank God with all my heart for healing Len! Now this is happening, after all this time! I love Len so much!"

Paul hugged Sandy and said, "Congratulations!"

Thelma and Tom also came up and hugged her. Thelma said, "I am so thankful that you and Len will finally be getting married. I never stopped praying that it would happen someday!"

"Thank you so much for praying for us for all these years. We haven't decided on a date yet or who else will be in the wedding, but we will let you know. Take care! Bye, bye!" She went back to her parents house. They also were so very happy that Sandy and Len would soon be getting married."

Chapter 16

As the summer went by, Caleb, Mary Ruth, and Tammy learned so much more from Pastor Ben. They wrote everything down, studied, learned it, and taught it to their friends, they also sent it to Ray.

In the group they were teaching was Henry and Jake, the two boys that had once been close friends with Mike, when they helped him beat Caleb up at school, quite awhile ago. They both changed tremendously but Mike would not come to them at all. Mike was still trying to cause trouble.

This coming year, Caleb and Mike would be seniors and Mary Ruth and Tammy would be freshmen in the same high school. They all really wanted to bring Mike to Jesus before they graduated.

After graduation, Caleb was planning to go to a Bible college and learn even more, which he could also teach to Tammy, Mary Ruth and Pepi.

Pepi was doing so good in learning from the Bible, mainly because he believed in it. He sent notes to Ray to read every week. Little did they know that Ray was really learning a lot also.

Pepi got a job at a grocery store. He worked full time and rented a small apartment close to where Caleb and Mary Ruth lived.

In September, Caleb celebrated his seventeenth birthday. Mary Ruth had already turned fourteen in July. They had a good year at school, but unfortunally, they were unable to have Mike come to them. The others also tried but it didn't work for them either.

Sandy and Len planed to get married on June 21st. Len was now completely normal and working again at the police station. He was not driving a police car yet, he was just working at the desk. He knew that he would soon be on the road again.

He had asked Paul to be his best man and Sandy asked Thelma to be her maid of honor. Thelma was so thrilled that Sandy asked her.

Sandy bought a beautiful wedding gown and Thelma and Mary Ruth each had beautiful yellow dresses. Of course, Len, Paul, and Caleb were going to wear beautiful tuxedoes.

It was now the beginning of May. They sent the wedding invitations to many people that they knew.

Sandy had her bridal shower in June and Len had his bachelor party. With all the things that were going on with their wedding, they definitely had a wonderful graduation party for Caleb.

Sandy and Len were still thinking about buying a house, which they probably could afford, but they didn't have enough money to buy all the things they would need for it. They would want new appliances and furniture plus many other things. They decided to stay at her parents home until they had enough money saved.

In September, Caleb would be starting his Bible college and turning eighteen. He now had his drivers license, thanks to Paul, and so did Pepi. Pepi didn't have a car, but Caleb's grandparents had bought him a used car for his birthday. Now, he can come home whenever he wants to because he wasn't going that far away for his teachings.

Mary Ruth and Tammy would now be going into tenth grade. Pepi was still working hard at the grocery store and doing a good job.

Sandy and Len's wedding would now be in two weeks. Everyone was looking forward to it and were all praying that it would be a wonderful and peaceful day. The marriage would take place at Sandy's First Baptist church.

They had decided to go to the Bahamas for their honeymoon. At first, they were thinking that they shouldn't go there because of what happened to them a few years ago when they left Nassau. Their plane had crashed on an island pretty far away, but the Lord had rescued them. They then thought, it surly wasn't the Bahama islands fault as to what happened to us, so they decided to go to Naussa for the week of their honeymoon. This time they were going on a ship!

The big day finally came! The weather was beautiful and the church was fully packed. Sandy's sister and her husband were also there. They had Pastor Ben, with her minister Pastor Samuel, performing their wedding together.

Len, Paul, and Caleb were standing up front with the ministers as the music started.

First, Mary Ruth, walked in smiling and holding a beautiful bouquet of flowers and went to the front. Then Thelma came up the isle. She was dressed the same as Mary Ruth and also had beautiful flowers.

When Thelma reached the front, the music changed to, "Here Comes The Bride!" In came Sandy with her father, Josh.. She looked like a beautiful angel heading to Len. Everyone started clapping as they got together. As she stood aside of Len, Josh hugged her and sat down with Jane. They were so happy that this was finally happening They both had tears of happiness running from their eyes.

Pastor Ben and Pastor Samuel began the marriage ceremony. Thelma reached over and put Sandy's veil behind her head. Sandy and Len each spoke their loving vows and put their wedding rings on each other.

Together, the two Pastors said, "We now pronounce you husband and wife. You may kiss the bride!"

Len and Sandy hugged and gave each other a big kiss. Everyone stood up and clapped. Caleb, Mary Ruth, Paul, Thelma, and the pastors all hugged and kissed them. Everyone was so happy!

They had their reception at the church. There were many pictures taken. They had great food in a buffet where everyone got in line to get their food, then sat at a table.

A local band was playing and many people were dancing. When the next song started, Pastor Ben went out and said to everyone, "Here to dance is Mr. and Mrs. Len Gordon. In a couple of minutes, they will be joined by Sandy's parent's, Jane and Josh Phillips, then Caleb and Mary Ruth Powell, Thelma Bailey and Paul Legna."

The music started, Len and Sandy danced for a few minutes, then were joined by the others. After a few more minutes, everyone was allowed to join them. They all had a wonderful time, even Tammy and Pepi were dancing.

When the next song came, Caleb asked Tammy to dance. He felt so good holding her in his arms. He didn't know it, but Tammy felt the same. They all had a wonderful time.

Len and Sandy were leaving for their honeymoon the next day. They were driving to Miami and getting on the ship to go to Nassau.

The ship was so nice.

When they arrived in Nassau, they took a cab to a beautiful hotel where they were staying for the week. They had a great time.

Len took Sandy around the town as Tom had taken him. He also took her to their favorite restaurant. The same male waiter was still working there and the second he saw Len, he came over, hugged him and said, "Hello, how are you? Long time, no see!" Len smiled and introduced him to his wife, Sandy, and they had a wonderful meal.

The next day he took her to the sheriff's office and introduced Sandy to Captain Como. Captain Coma said to Len, "How great to see you again with your new wife! How is Caleb and Mary Ruth doing?" Len told him how they were and also that Pepi was with them now.

"Well, that's a surprise! He was being taken care of here by the man who owns a great restaurent downtown named Manuel Torres. We couldn't find any relatives of Pepi's. Manuel Torres was going to keep Pepi, but suddenly, he disappeared. We searched for him for quite awhile, but never did find him. We never found out what happened, but now we kind of know what must have taken place. I'll have to get with Mr. Torres and let him know that Pepi is alright and that he is in Florida. I wonder how he got there?"

Len told the Captain about the robbery that Pepi was accused of and what happened. After he was released from prison, he lived with Caleb and Mary Ruth for awhile. He is now working in a grocery store and learning more and more about the Bible from Caleb, Mary Ruth, their friend named, Tammy, and her grandfather, pastor Ben.

"Boy, that's really great that those young people are walking in the path of the Lord," replied Captain Como.

"It was really great seeing you again, especially for no problem, take care and if you ever come to St. Cloud, Florida, come and see us!"

"You bet I will! Take care and have a wonderful marriage. Bye." Sandy and Len then went and spent the rest of the day at the beach.

The next day, they took a tour of the island, went shopping, and had a great time. They really enjoyed Nassau.

Sandy said, "I can't help but think that this is going to be a really popular place in the future."

"I certainly agree," replied Len.

Their honeymoon went by so fast and finally the last day came. They got back on the ship and headed for Miami. When they arrived, they got in their car and started driving back to St. Cloud.

When they got home, they sat down with Sandy's parents and told them what a great time they had in Nassau. They also gave them some presents.

"Now we have to start saving money so we can buy a house, " said Sandy.

"We love you both, as far as I'm concerned, you both can stay here forever," Jane said.

"We love you and Josh too, but do you really want us and ten little kids here?" asked Len.

They all laughed, but Sandy just stared and smiled a little bit. Len asked, "Sandy, what's wrong?"

"I don't know if I can take care of ten kids," she replied.

Len hugged her and said, "Sandy, I was only kidding when I said ten kids!"

Sandy smiled and said, "I know you were. Ten kids would be a lot!" They went to bed and had a nice time together. When they were finished, Len gave her a big kiss, rolled over, and fell asleep.

Sandy couldn't fall asleep, she kept thinking of what happened in her past. No one knows what happened except my sister and her husband. Should I tell Len and my parents what happened? I have to make a decision. They might hate me if I tell them. At least my sister, Judy, and her husband, John, never said a word about it.

Chapter 17

Mary Ruth had her 15th birthday on July 31st, and Caleb turned 18 on Septermber 15th. On September 5th was Thelma's birthday and their great uncle, Pastor Ben. They had nice parties and lots of fun.

Caleb started his Bible college and Mary Ruth started 10th grade that month. Her and Tammy were now doing so much. Besides teaching about the Lord, they were doing all they could to help others. They truly loved everyone. Everyone was so proud of them!

Caleb came home on weekends. They had a wonderful Bible study with all their friends on Saturdays and went to Pastor Ben's church on Sundays. Caleb loved his college and was learning more and more.

Pepi was doing fine. He was now, already, one of the assistance managers at the grocery store and making a little more money. He already bought a 1966 Ford Mustang. That way he was able to take Mary Ruth and Tammy wherever they wanted to go when he wasn't working. He also helped them help others.

Paul was doing good. He visited everyone often and kept in touch.

One Friday in November, Tammy and Mary Ruth were walking together. Tammy was going to spend the night with Mary Ruth. They planned to get up early on Saturday morning and go to Jane's church and help them make Christmas stockings full of useful things to give to the poor people in the area. It was cold but they both has jackets on.

As they turned the corner to Lake Shore Blvd., they heard a strange noise. It sounded like several dogs crying. They walked toward the fence in the yard aside of them.. It was dark, but they could see a man with a whip hitting the dogs. They had no idea who the man was as there was only a small porch light on.

Mary Ruth said, "Tammy, I'm going to stop that man!"

Before Tammy could say anything, Mary Ruth jumped over the fence and ran toward the man screaming, "Stop it! Stop hurting the dogs!"

Next thing she knew, the man turned to her and hit her with the whip. He hurt her legs and she fell on the ground.

Tammy saw what happened. She didn't know what to do. She thought, what if that man is going to kill Mary Ruth? As Tammy ran around to the other side of the fence, the man was standing over Mary Ruth with the whip held up. Mary Ruth legs were hurting so bad, she was unable to move.

The man yelled, "Who do you think you are?" Suddenly, the voice sounded very familiar to Mary Ruth.

Then the man yelled again, "You have no right to be in my yard!" He picked the whip up and was about to hit her body really hard, when all of a sudden, Tammy was behind him and hit him on the head with a large rock she found in the yard.

He fell down and was unconscious. Tammy helped Mary Ruth up and helped her get to the gate. Tammy opened the gate and they went out. Behind them ran the three dogs.

Tammy helped Mary Ruth to her home. Mary Ruth had a hard time trying to walk. She was in pain. They finally made it. Tammy knocked on the door and Thelma opened it. She cried, "Oh no! What happened?"

Tom heard her and ran over to them. Mary Ruth said, "Granny, I just fell and hurt my legs real bad."

Thelma and Tom raised the bottom of her slacks up and looked at her legs. Tom said, "Come on, let's take her to the hospital and have them checked. They all got in the car and went to the hospital.

At the emergency room, they x- rayed her legs and only one was broken. The doctor said, "This could have been a lot worse than it is. It was only a slight break." They wrapped the broken leg up, gave her crutches and some pain pills.

As they were going home, Thelma asked Mary Ruth, "What exactly happened? How did you break your leg?"

"Tammy and I were just running and jumping and I fell off the curb," replied Mary Ruth.

"Well, you better not do that any more because it could happen again. Thank God it isn't to bad!" said Tom.

When they got to the house, Tammy and Mary Ruth had a little bit to eat, Mary Ruth took a pain pill, then they went up to her room.

Tammy asked, "Why did you lie to your grandparents? You know we're not supposed to lie!"

"I know I told a lie and I asked God to forgive me. One time Caleb lied. Only because he wanted to save three boys and bring them to accept the Lord. Two of them did come and received our Lord and Savior and also joined our group. The other boy wouldn't come no matter what. We tried and tried for years to bring him to the Lord. We felt so bad and prayed that someday it would work out. I believe the time is coming now."

"Why would you be thinking that now?" Tammy asked.

"Because the man who was hurting the dogs and hit me with the whip, is that boy, Mike! The boy who would never listen to us!"

"Oh my, I can see why you didn't tell your grandmother what really happened!"

"Yes, they might have called the police and who knows what would have happened then? Caleb will be here tomorrow morning. I have to tell him what happened and we can decide how to handel it."

The next morning, Caleb arrived early and had breakfast with them and his grandparents. After breakfast, Caleb, Mary Ruth and Tammy went out on the porch.

When Caleb arrived, everyone was sitting at the table. He was very surprised when Mary Ruth got up and walked out with crutches. They sat down and Caleb asked, "Mary Ruth, what happened?"

She told him that her leg was only slightly broken and then told him the whole story and that the young man was Mike. She also told him that she told a lie about what happened to her grandparents.

Caleb said, "This might be a good time to bring Mike to our Lord and Savior. How about I get with Paul and tell him the whole story. I really feel that he will be able to work with us. I always remember how he spoke of the Lord when we were on the island."

"I remember that also. When I think of him, I never saw him do anything sinful or even tell a lie. When we were on the island and I was only seven years old, I used to think that he might be an angel and appeared on the island to help us. He still helps us," replied Mary Ruth.

"I understand your feelings for him. He has always helped us so much. Come to think of it, we don't even know anything about his previous life. All I know is that we love him and thank God that he came to us when he did. Anyway, I'm going to call him and ask him if we can see him and tell him this whole story."

"I'm sure he will help us and come up with a good idea of what to do," said Mary Ruth.

A little while later, Thelma and Tom were going to the grocery store. Thelma said, "We don't usually go on a Saturday, but we're out of so many things that I need for what I'm planing to make tonight. See you all later!"

They left and Caleb said, "Now is a good time to call Paul at work." An officer answered the phone and Caleb asked him if he would give Paul a message.

"Of course I will, but I won't see him until Monday. He's off this weekend. You can call him at his house."

Calb thanked the officer and was so glad that Paul was off this weekend. He called Paul and explained to him that he, Mary Ruth and Tammy wanted to come over and talk to him about something very important.

"No problem! I would love to be with you all again," Paul replied.

Tammy called Jane and told her that they wouldn't be able to come over this morning because Mary Ruth had broken her leg. Jane told her to tell Mary Ruth that she is so sorry she broke her leg and not to worry because she couldn't help her today.

They got in Caleb's car and went right over to Paul's. They went in his home and hugged him.

Paul said, "Have a seat. Would any of you like some ice tea or soda?"

"We're fine, let me tell you this whole story that started years ago when Mary Ruth and I were in elementary school. That was after we had gotten off the island and came here." He and Mary Ruth told him the whole story.

"I was wondering why Mary Ruth was on crutches. This Mike seemes like he is being ruled by Satan! I've seen things like this that have happened in the past. Do you want to go over this afternoon and see if he's there?"

"We sure do!"

"Well, let's talk about what we are going to do if he is there. I'm going to take you all to lunch, we'll talk, then we'll go over to his house."

After lunch they went over to the house where Mike had been hitting the dogs. Paul told Mary Ruth and Tammy to stay in the car while him and Caleb tried to talk to Mike.

Paul and Caleb went over and knocked on the door and right away Mike opened it. He looked at them and said, "What do you want Caleb and who's this guy?"

"The main reason I came here now is because you broke my sister's leg."

Mike just looked at him and said, "I don't have any idea what your talking about!"

"Last night when you were hurting your dogs, Mary Ruth tried to stop you. Then you hit her with a whip and broke her leg."

"Oh really, I didn't have any idea who that girl was, but she had no business coming into my yard. Then, somehow, I was hit on the head with a big rock. I have no idea who tried to kill me."

"That girl was not trying to kill you, she was trying to save Mary Ruth because you were going to beat her more with the whip!" Caleb replied.

"Look, just get out of here and leave me alone! You can't prove what I did!" At that moment, Paul interrupted and said, "My name is Paul Legna, I'm a police officer here in St. Cloud and I just heard you more or less admit how you hurt Mary Ruth. The other girl is also a witness as to what you were doing. Would you like to be arrested now?"

Mike was shocked. He slammed the door in their face. Paul kicked it in, then he and Caleb entered the house. The house was a mess! There were things laying everywhere. They then went into the kitchen, looking for Mike. There were pots, pans, plates, silverware and old food all over the place. They didn't have any idea where Mike went.

Suddenly, they noticed him through the kitchen window. He was on the back porch. When they entered the back porch, Paul said to Mike, "Did you come to a decision?"

Caleb then said, "Mike, I can give you another decision to make. If you promise to come to us and behave, we can teach you about the Lord and how he will forgive your sins."

Mike was really mad. If Paul wasn't a police officer, he would have fought with them. He knew that he was very strong, as he had beaten many people up before, including Caleb.

Mike finally said, "Okay, I will come to your teachings, only because I don't want to go to jail again. I'm not even going to listen to what you are teaching me!"

Paul replied, "You better listen and be nice to them. I plan on giving you a test in a month, if you don't pass it, I will arrest you because Mary Ruth will still be on her crutches."

Caleb also told Mike that he would take him to church for the next month, plus he will have a teaching on Saturdays from 3 PM to 4 PM and on Tuesday and Thursday nights at 7 to 9 PM. He has to go to Mary Ruth's home and be with the teaching group during the week and I will be there on Saturdays.

Paul asked, "Well, what's your decision? Will you do everything Caleb said, or go to jail?"

"Yes, I will do it, but will it be over in a month?"

"Yes, you won't be arrested and you will only come to the Lord if you decide to."

"I know that I can last a month, then I'll be on my way. I might just leave this town and go somewhere better. I also want this in writing so you can't keep me with you."

"Okay it's a deal. We will pick you up tomorrow morning and you, I, and the girls will go to church. Be ready at 9AM as we are going to the Christ Lutheran church in Kissimmee where my great uncle, Pastor Ben Wylie preaches," replied Caleb.

Paul went to shake Mike's hand, but he pulled away. Caleb said, "Goodbye, see you tomorrow."

Paul and Caleb got in the car where Mary Ruth and Tammy were waiting. Mary Ruth asked, "What happened?"

Paul said, "He finally agreed to go to church and Bible studies with all of you, rather than being arrested."

"We now have to do our very best to have him understand and accept our wonderful Lord and Savior. I fell that a demon is with him. He acts so terrible all the time. His house is a disaster, everything is a wreck, but I don't think that he cares about anything," replied Caleb.

Tammy asked, "Does anyone live with him?"

"I don't know, but I doubt it. We have to do our best to help him in many ways."

"I've never been to your uncle's church, can I go with you all tomorrow? We can pick Mike up together," asked Paul.

Caleb said, "I think that would be a great idea!"

Mike was sitting on his back porch thinking. I don't want to be with Caleb and the girls for a month. Maybe I can get out of it. Maybe I can have them get in a wreck! Then they won't be trying to change anyone! That's what I'll do on the way to church! I'll jump out of the car before it crashes!"

Chapter 18

The next morning at 9AM Mike heard the car's horn beeping in front of his house. He was dressed like he was going to go hunting, not to church. He walked down to the car and got in. He was shocked to see that he was now sitting next to Paul. He thought, Oh no! I didn't think that Paul would be here! I guess for now I just better behave and go to church with them, or I will be really put in jail if I cause an accident and Paul survives.

When they got to the church, they took Mike to Pastor Ben's office and introduced him to the pastor. Mike still did not smile or shake hands, even with a pastor.

Pastor Ben said, "I saved you all some seats in the front row so you can hear my sermon." [Caleb had called him the night before and told him the whole story about Mike.]

Pastor Ben looked at Mike and said, "I hope you like this church." Mike just looked away.

"I'm sure I will! When we leave here, I'm going to ask Mike what the sermon was about and I know he will be able to tell me." said Paul.

Mile thought, Oh no, now I better listen!

As the church service started, they sang several hymms, then Pastor Ben and everyone prayed. He then started his sermon about how we have an awesome Lord who gives power and strength to his people. How you can count on God's help when you are tired and have nothing to offer, when your in pain, or sick, or when your tempted. If you believe in love, and have faith in the Lord, you do not need to be in fear or stress. He will strengthen you if you trust in him.

You must receive God's blessings through Christ. Through Christ, God has blessed us with every spiritual blessing that He has to offer.

You must believe in God's Son, Jesus Christ, out Lord and Savior, and be reborned in Him. Then God is ready to give blessings to all who come to him through his Son. We rejoice in our wonderful new relationship with God all because of what the Lord, Jesus Christ has done for us in dying on the cross so our sins would be forgiven.

Roman's 8:32 says, "He who did not withold or spare even His own Son, but gave Him up for us all, will He not also with Him freely and graciously give us all other things?" Only faith can gaurentee the blessings that we hope for."

The Lord is an ever lasting God. He never grows tired or weary. He strengthens those who are weak and tired.

Mike was listening to this and thinking, I never heard of these things before. I wonder if they're true? At least I listened to the sermon and will be able to answer anything that Paul asks me. Only three more Sundays to go! Then they'll leave me alone and I can do whatever I feel like. To bad I have quite a few Bible studies to attend. I never even had a Bible, let alone read it. How do I know if what it says is really true?

The sermon ended and a few more songs were sung to the Lord. A prayer was said by Pastor Ben, then the sevice ended. Everyone was hugging each other and shaking hands. Mike just walked out of the church. Paul was right behind him and said, "Where do you think your going?

"No where. I'm just waiting for you all to come out and take me home."

"You probably don't realize this, but Christian people love each other and help those in need." He then started asking Mike questions about the sermon. He was very surprised that Mike was answering very good.

Paul thought, This boy is not dumb. If he can remember the sermon, hopefully it will stay in his mind. At least we're having a good start.

In about twenty minutes, Caleb, Mary Ruth, Tammy, Pepi, Thelma, and Tom came out of the church.

Mike got in the car with Caleb, Pepi, and Paul and they took him home. When they got there, Caleb said, "Don't forget to go to my home on Tuesday night at 7PM for Mary Ruth and Tammy's Bible study.

Paul said, "Don't worry, I'll call him on the phone and remind him, as I will be at work, otherwise, I would have picked him up and taken him there."

"Thank you so much. I really appreciate you doing that," replied Caleb.

Mike just looked at them, rolled his eyes, and got out of the car. Paul said, "Don't worry, I'll remind you about the Bible study on Tuesday." Mike just turned around, got out of the car and went in his house.

As they were driving to Caleb's house, Paul told them how Mike was able to answer most of the questions he asked him about the sermon.

"That sounds really good. I have to tell that to Mary Ruth and Tammy and remind them to teach Mike great things at the Bible study for him to think about and hopefully remember."

When they got to Caleb's home, they invited Paul for lunch with them. After he ate he got in his truck and went home.

Caleb said to Tammy and Mary Ruth, "Mike is going to be with you at your Bible studies on Tuesdays and Thursdays. I wrote all the times and days of the studies and gave it to him so he wouldn't be able to say that he forgot. In fact Paul will be calling him. Please try not to be afraid of him when he comes."

"We won't worry, because all of our friends will be there. No matter how tuff Mike thinks he is, he'll never beat up twenty people," replied Tammy. "The Lord will also be with us."

Mary Ruth said, "That's right, I'm sure they will all try to help him understand what we are saying."

On Tuesday night, they thought that Mike might not be coming, but he did show up twenty minutes late. When Mike knocked on the door, Tammy answered it. She smiled at him and said, "Welcome." She took him in the living room where everyone was and introduced him to all of them. All the boys and girls there were in high school. They saved a special seat for Mike and showed it to him.

Mary Ruth said, "We already said our prayer but we surly don't mind doing it again. Mike, we all hold hands and bow our heads." They all held hands again. Mike held Mary Ruth's hand and a boy named Luke.

"DEAR LORD, PLEASE BE WITH US AND HELP US TO LEARN MORE AND MORE FROM THE BIBLE. WE KNOW THAT YOU ALWAYS HELP US AND WE ARE SO THANKFUL

TO YOU. WE HAVE FAITH IN YOU AND ALWAYS WILL. PLEASE BE WITH OUR NEW MEMBER, MIKE, AND HELP HIM WANT TO BE REBORNED IN YOUR SON, JESUS CHRIST, OUR WONDERFUL LORD AND SAVIOR. IN JESUS HOLY NAME, AMEN."

They all sat down again, Mike kept his face down and refused to look at anyone.

Mary Ruth started the study and said, "You all know that we need not worry about anything if we believe in the Lord and have true faith in Him and what He did for us on the cross. We will pray. We should tell God what we need and thank Him for all He does for us.

If you do this, you will experience God's peace which is far more wonderful than the human mind can understand. His peace will guard your hearts and minds, as you live in Jesus Christ."

Tammy then started talking, "The key to inner peace is prayer. God is a Father, not a force. We can connect with God because He is a caring Father.

Psalms 103:13 says, "As a father has compassion on his children, so the Lord has compassion in those who honor Him."

"He also is a consistant Father. He is never to busy for us and He loves to meet our needs."

Mary Ruth then said, "He is also sympathetic to our hurts. He is our complete Father. God sent Jesus to make the connection. Jesus said, "I am the way, the truth, and the life. No one comes to the Father except through Me. If you would really know Me, you would know my Father as well."

"Yes, we are the children of God through faith in Jesus Christ," said Tammy.

Everyone but Mike smiled and said, "Amen."

They all started talking about how they were raised when they were young children. Some had religious families and some did not. They talked about how they now prayed, where they would go to pray, and how often they prayed.

Mary Ruth then asked, "Did the Lord help you with anything in your life?" The boys and girls started telling her things that they knew the Lord was helping them with.

Mary Ruth them looked over at Mike. His head was still down and she thought, I pray that he is paying attention and learning about God and His Son Jesus Christ

When the study was over, they prayed again and thanked the Lord for their Bible study.

Mary Ruth said to Mike, "See you on Thursday!" Mike didn't even look at her or say anything, just walked out of the door.

"We need to pray a lot for Mike," said Tammy.

"I truly believe that. I wonder if he will ever apologize for breaking my leg?" asked Mary Ruth. "I hope he shows up on Thursday."

Thursday night's Bible study came and Tammy and Mary Ruth were surprised to see that Mike was there on time, although he didn't smile or say hello to anyone. He just sat down on his chair. He did hold hands while Tammy said the prayer.

Mary Ruth started by saying, "Today we're going to study about how to manage your mouth. Why must we watch what we say? There are several reasons. My tongue directs where I go. My tongue can destroy what I have. In Proverbs 21:23 it says, "If you want to stay out of trouble be careful what you say."

My tongue displays who I am. Everyone should be quick to listen, slow to speak, and slow to become angry. We are not to lie, but be honest and truthful."

Tammy said, "You can try to help people but don't yell at them if they do something wrong. Help people when you talk to them, don't make them upset or nervous. Do not curse or say bad words. Love everyone, help them in their needs."

"Yes, save them and bring them to the Lord," said Mary Ruth.

Mike was still looking down, but he did lift his eyes a little bit and glanced at Mary Ruth. He lowered his eyes and thought, I know that they're probably speaking these things for me. Why would they want to help me when they know how I am? One time I bet Caleb up and now I broke his sister's leg. You think that they would really hate me and not want anything to do with me.

All of a sudden, something came into his mind and said, "They do hate you! Don't trust them! Their probably going to kill you when they get a chance!"

Then Mike thought, Why am I even here? I probably would have done better in jail! I don't trust any of these boys and girls!

Suddenly, he got up and left. Everybody just looked at each other. Nobody had any idea why he left. At the end of the Bible study, they prayed for Mike and that he would come back to them.

After everyone left, Mary Ruth and Tammy went up to her bedroom. Tammy always spent the night with Mary Ruth on the nights of the Bible studies. They started talking about Mike.

Tammy said, "Why did he just get up and leave? Did we say something wrong?"

"No, I know we were talking about the right thing, especially for him. I think that something strange happened to him. I sure hope he comes on Saturday when Caleb is here. Caleb is so very intelligent when it comes to the Bible. I think the Lord is teaching him even more then the human flesh can." They prayed again, then went to sleep.

On Saturday morning, Caleb arrived. He first asked Mary Ruth how her leg was doing. Mary Ruth told him that she was doing fine, thanks to the Lord.

Mary Ruth and Tammy then told him what happened at the Bible study on Thursday with Mike.

Caleb said, "I don't think that he's going to show up today. I'm going to go over to his house. I want to talk to him. I wish Paul was able to come with me, but I know that he's at work this weekend."

"Let me and Tammy come with you!"

"Mary Ruth, you're still on crutches and the boys and girls will be coming here for the Bible study. You and Tammy just pray for me."

"Caleb, please let me come with you! I don't want you to be alone with Mike, and I'm not on crutches! Mary Ruth can teach the Bible study. Plese let me come!" cried Tammy.

"Okay, you can come, but if Mike starts fighting with me, I want you to run over to a neighbors and call the police."

Mary Ruth cried, "We will all pray for you both until you come back!"

Tammy and Caleb got into his car and drove over to Mike's house. When they knocked on the door, Mike opened it and said, "Get out of here! I don't want to be with you anymore!"

"We just want to talk to you," stated Caleb.

Mike then thought, I'll let them come in, and they will be sorry! He then said, "Okay, come in."

They sat down in the living room and Mike said, "Just a minute, I'm going to the kitchen to get us something to drink."

Tammy and Caleb didn't want to upset him so they didn't say anything. In a few minutes he came back with a tray and three glasses of soda on it. He set it on the table.

The next second, he ran behind Tammy. He had a sharp knife in his hand and held it in front of her neck. Tammy started to cry.

Caleb jumped up and shouted. "Let Tammy alone! Tammy never bothered you! I'm the one you hated for years!" Caleb kept talking to Mike. Suddenly, Mike left Tammy go and came at Caleb with the knife.

Tammy ran out the door, she was crying and praying that Caleb wouldn't be killed. As she ran toward the neighbor's house, she saw a police care come around the corner. She scramed and waved at the police car. The officer pulled off the road and jumped out. It was Paul!!!

Tammy ran up to him and screamed, "Mike is going to kill Caleb over in that house!"

Paul ran in the door and Tammy followed him. Caleb was on the floor and Mike was on top of him with the knife in the air, heading for Caleb's heart!

Paul ran over and grabbed Mike by the neck. Mike dropped the knife and Tammy picked it up. Caleb jumped up, then he and Paul knocked Mike on the floor and held him down.

Mike yelled, "Get off of me! I thought you were supposed to be nice people!"

Paul shouted, "We're not getting off of you until you settle down!"

Caleb said, "I believe there is a demon in you and he is having you think bad thoughts."

Suddenly something said in Mike's mind, "Don't listen to them!"

Mike then yelled, "I'm not going to listen to anything you say to me!"

Paul asked, "Did something just tell you that in your mind?"

Mike thought, How does he know that something like that could happen?

"If you would learn the Bible, you would understand how Satan can have you do wrong! You must learn how to keep Satan from controlling your life!" Tammy cried.

"The three of us are now going to pray for you that the Lord will take the demon out of you!" cried Paul.

They all started praying to the Lord for Mike. As they were praying, Mike was trying to get up. Then he started screaming and crusing. Caleb, Paul and Tammy continued to pray for twenty minute as Mike continued to try to get away and to scream and curse at them.

All of a sudden, Mike stopped moving and screaming! He looked like he was unconscious. Caleb stopped holding him and touched his face. "Mike, wake up, are you okay?"

Mike opened his eyes and looked at them. He asked, "What happened?"

"We prayed that whatever was making you sin and not want you to learn about and believe in Jesus Christ would leave you. I believe it did! How are you feeling?" asked Paul.

"I feel so different than I usually feel. I feel calm and peaceful."

Caleb asked, "Do you feel that you want your sins forgiven? Or would you rather wait until we teach you more?"

"Believe it or not, at this moment, I feel very different than I always am. I do want my sins forgiven and I never want to sin again, like I did before! I don't know why I feel so different!"

"We feel that there was a demon in you making you do all those bad things, but now the Lord has made him leave you."

Mike asked, "Will he ever come back?"

"Yes, he can come back and again try to change you. He can make you stressed out and worried, can make you say or do wrong things. There are many things he will try to do to you to make you do bad things."

"We will teach you about it. You must have complete faith and love in Jesus Christ and God His Father. If you believe in Jesus Christ, your sins will be forgiven and you can be with God, His Father, through Him. Also, you will be baptized with the Holy Spirit and He will help you."

Mike cried, "I want my sins forgiven!"

Paul said, "Repeat after me, Dear Jesus, I repent of my sins {Mike repeats after Paul says a few words} and accept You as my Lord and Savior. Please help me walk in your path of righteousness and do Your will."

They helped him up and put him on the couch. Mike looked at them and said, "Thank you all so much for helping me and I pray that I will be a good person and a loving Christian. Please teach me and let me be with you and help you bring others to Jesus. I feel so different! It is so wonderful and I thank you again and again for helping me, after seeing me do bad things now and in the past years I had no idea that a demon could be in me having me do those bad things"

Paul said, "I just want to tell you that if you start thinking bad thoughts about anything, it could be Satan trying to get you back to do his will and be a bad person instead of a good Christian person. The more faithful you are to God, the more Satan will try to change you. You never know what he will try to do to you. You must keep your faith and do God's will."

Mike replied, "If I start thinking bad thoughts, can I come over for help?"

"Of course you can!" said Tammy.

Caleb asked, "Would you like to come over now and be with us for awhile? Mary Ruth is doing the Bible study for me right now. I had no idea what would happen when we came over to you. I am so thankful to the Lord that He was with us and helped you."

"I thank the Lord with all my heart for ridding me of my evilness and bringing me to Jesus Christ. I promise that I will never leave Him," cried Mike.

They all put their hands on Mike and Paul said, "God bless you. We all love you and want you to be with Caleb, Mary Ruth, Tammy, and Pepi from now on."

Caleb said, "Come on, let's go to my house. Thank you, Paul, for helping us. I don't know what would have happened if you hadn't been here. I know that the Lord brought you here to help us."

Paul smiled and said, "I believe your right! I'm going back to work now. Take care and have a great day!"

They all hugged him and said, "Bye, see you soon!"

Caleb, Tammy and Mike got in the car and went to Caleb's house. When they got there, Mary Ruth, Pepi and all the others were just finishing their Bible study. When Mary Ruth looked over and saw that Mike was with them, she was shocked. She didn't think that he would come to the Bible study, but prayed he would.

Mike walked over to Mary Ruth and hugged her. He said, "I am so sorry that I hurt you and was so mean to you and everyone else all these years. Please forgive me!"

Mary Ruth smiled and said "I do forgive you!" All the others cried, "I do forgive you too!"

The Bible study was over. Mary Ruth said a prayer and said, "See you all on Tuesday night." As they were leaving, Mike hugged everyone and thanked them for forgiving him. Caleb then told Mary Ruth and Pepi what happened.

Pepi said, "Thank you Dear Lord! I don't know Mike but I did hear things about him. It is so wonderful that he completely changed and accepted Jesus Christ as his Lord and Savior! That is awesome! I went through kind of the same thing. I will tell you, Mike, about it someday and how I came to the Lord." They then decided since Mike was there, to study the chapter of Luke in the new testament.

When they were done studying, Mike said, "That is so great, to start learning about Jesus! I am so happy! I promise that I will be going to church with you every Sunday and I will be with you at every Bible study forever!"

"Come on, I'll take you and Tammy home," Caleb said. He dropped Mike off and took Tammy to her house. They sat in the car and talked about the wonderful thing that happened this day.

Tammy said, "See you tomarrow at church." As she was about to get out of the car, Caleb hugged her and said "Bye, bye."

As Tammy got out of the car, she thought, Caleb hardly ever hugs me, but it was really nice of him!"

The next day at church, Pastor Ben, Thelma, Tom, and Tammy's parents were amazed at the change in Mike. He was smiling at everyone, and being a very nice person. They all were so thankful and so was Mike!

Chapter 19

Sandy and Len were having a great marriage. They were still living with Sandy's parents. It was really nice, but they wanted to get their own home.

Caleb and Mary Ruth came over a lot and told them all the things that were happening with them.

Sandy, Len and her parents were so glad that Tammy was their best friend and that Pepi was now with them. They were really happy to hear that Mike had changed so much and that he truly accepted Jesus Christ as his Lord and Savior. They also knew how wonderful it was that Caleb and Mary Ruth were teaching the Bible and having more young people be reborn in Jesus.

Caleb and Mary Ruth then told them about all their Bible studies and how Caleb was learning much more in his Bible college.

One night when Sandy and Len went to bed, Len hugged her and said, "Just think, we're married six months already! We are also saving a lot of money. It won't be to much longer until we can start looking for our house. I can't wait to start having kids!"

Sandy looked at him and said, "Me too." She then turned over and shut her eyes.

In the next two years, everything was still going well with everyone. Tammy and Mary Ruth graduated from high school and Caleb had only a short time to be graduated from his college.

Caleb had fallen in love with Tammy although he didn't let her know. Caleb thought, Now that she is out of high school, I'm hoping that we can become closer.

They were doing so well with their Bible studies and bringing more young people to Jesus. Not only did they become helpers of all the needy people in the area, they were planing to go into more counties. Pepi and Mike were getting more knowledgeable about the Bible and being with Caleb, Mary Ruth and Tammy in teaching.

Sandy and Len now had a beautiful house that was on the same street as Jane and Josh. For some reason, Sandy still hadn't gotten pregnant. Len couldn't understand why and Sandy told him she had no idea why.

One day Pepi got a phone call. It was Raymond Hopkins, the man he was in the cell with when he was in prison. Pepi was excited to hear from him and asked, "How are you doing? It's been such a long time since we talked! I hope you are still studying your Bible."

"Pepi, I sure have been since you left and still am. I am so glad that you gave me that Bible and the glasses that allowed me to be able to read it. You'll be excited when I tell you what happened! About six months after you left, I got with the warden and asked him if I could get with some people at lunch time and teach them some things that are in the Bible. He said, Sure, we'll give you some extra time to be with them. One of the officers will take you all back to everyone's cells when you're finished. We'll give you an hour. Then he said, "Good Luck!"

"I only had three other men come to my little Bible study, but they all were very interested in learning. I was able to learn so much more with the notes you all sent me. A few weeks later, two more men came. Within three months, I had twenty men in my class! It was amazing! The next thing that happened, the prison bought twenty Bibles and gave them to the men to read. They were able to read their own Bibles now instead of just listening to me.

Next thing that happened was a local Christian minister, named Zac Davis, came over and helped me teach. Actually, he taught me much more than I knew. It was great. He used to come an hour early and answer all the questions I had. Then more and more prisoners came to the group. Quite a few of them were reborn in Jesus Christ, as they asked that their sins be forgiven and accepted Him as their Lord and Savior. How wonderful it was!

I began to have some very good friends. Now two of my good friends are working with Pastor Zac."

Pepi said, "That is so wonderful, that happened in a prison because of you, but why did you stop teaching?"

Ray said, "Believe it or not, I was released from prison a week ago! My time was finished and now I'm in Orlando looking for a job."

"You do know that I'm in a Christain group with Caleb, Mary Ruth, Tammy, and a man named Mike. We are bringing others to the Lord and helping everyone with their problems and needs. How about on my next day off, I come up to Orlando and bring you down here to meet everyone"?

"That would be really nice. When can you come up?"

"I'm now off on the weekends. Now I'm able to go to and help at the Bible study on Saturday and go to church on Sunday. I have been working at Winn Dixie for over two years and now I'm the first assistant manager. It is a good job. We also have our other great friend with us, named Mike. He has a good job fixing cars. He's really great because he does help people who can't afford to have their cars fixed. Anyway, how about I pick you up on Saturday morning and you can come to our Bible study and meet everyone.

"I'm looking forward to it. I'm staying with my friend, Pete, who lives up here. The address is 114 Orange Avenue."

Pepi replied, "I'm so very glad for what you started in the prison and that you are now released. I'll see you around 8 o'clock on Saturday morning."

"I'll definitely be ready! I'm looking forward to it. I'm so glad that I was able to get in contact with you!"

When Pepi went to the Bible study on Thursday night, he told them about Ray and the Bible study he started at the prison, and how it got better and better. Then he told them that Ray had been released from prison and is staying in Orlando. He asked, "Is it okay with you all if I bring him down to attend out Bible study on Saturday?"

Caleb smiled and said, "Of course it is! He has done a wonderful thing at the prison and is with the Lord because of you, Pepi. We are really looking forward to seeing him." Caleb, Mary Ruth, Tammy,and Mike, all hugged Pepi.

Early Saturday morning, Pepi drove up to Orlando and went to the place where Ray was staying. He noticed Ray sitting on the porch.

Pepi got out of the car and ran over to him. They smiled and hugged each other. Pepi said, "Ray, you look great! Thank you for coming to our Bible study! I'm so glad to see you again!"

"I'm also looking forward to seeing Caleb and Mary Ruth! I know they helped you become a good Christian person, then you truly helped me. It is so wonderful to completely believe in our Lord, love Him, and have complete faith and trust in Him."

"Yes, said Pepi, that is the best thing that can happen in a person's life, to be reborn in Jesus Christ! We also should obey Him and do his will. He loves everyone and forgives their sins, but the Christians should realize that they should do their best never to sin again and keep the commandments of God."

"I agree 100%! We have to keep our flesh in the narrow path of His righteousness and not let out flesh or Satan take us out of it. I know it is hard to do but the Lord will help us. We must pray to him to lead us and guide us," replied Ray.

"Wow, you sure did leard and understand a lot! Let's go to St. Cloud." They got in the car and arrived at Caleb and Mary Ruth's house a while before the Bible study was to begin. Caleb, Mary Ruth, Tammy and Mike were there.

They all talked with Ray and were very impressed. Caleb said to himself, How great that a very nasty man who was in prison for doing wrong, was now a man of God!

When all the others arrived, they introduced Ray to them, then started the Bible study. When it ended, Ray said, "That was a great Bible study! It is so wonderful that you all are teaching these young people. All the young people should be taught everything in the Bible."

Tammy said, "We are planning to teach more plus help others who really need help. We're now planning to become missionaries and go to other states, even other countries if possible. We want to bring more and more people to the Lord."

"That is awesome! If it is possible, I would love to be with you all and teach others about our Lord," replied Ray.

"I only have a short time to go at my college, meanwhile, we'll do all we can for others in the state of Florida," said Caleb.

"If you want to come down here and be with our group, you can stay with me until you can find a job and are able to afford a place of your own," announced Pepi.

"I truly need to find a job ASAP. I have nothing. No clothes, except what I'm wearing, no car, no home, not even a family. I do have a toothbrush and touthpaste, but that's about it," replied Ray.

Pepi, Mary Ruth, Caleb, Tammy and Mike all put their hands on Ray and prayed for him. When they were finished, Mike said, "Come down and stay with Pepi, we will all give you things you need. I'm sure that you will fit in some of my clothes which I plan to give you."

Mary Ruth said, We will all truly help you with everything you need also. Tammy and I even went to Mike's house and cleaned the whole place. Mike was so thankful that we did that for him, he now keeps it clean himself."

"Yes, that was really wonderful of them! I never did anything since I inherited the house from my grandmother. It was clean when I got it, but because of how I was at that time, it wasn't clean for very long."

Ray then asked Mike, "Did you happen to previously lead a bad life like I did?

"I truly did, but I was saved by Caleb, Tammy and a police officer named Paul. They brought me back to a good life through our Lord and Savior."

Ray exclaimed, "Pepi basically did the same for me while we were in prison. I want to help others come to the Lord so very much!

Mike said, "Me too! I will never give up!"

Chapter 20

Sandy and Len were now married two years. They had their own beautiful home and it was only one block from her parents. They also had everything they needed and wanted inside. They loved their home.

One night as they sat on the couch watching TV, Len said to Sandy, "I can't understand why you haven't gotten pregnant yet. Do you have any idea what's stopping you?"

Sandy didn't even look at him and said, "No, I have no idea why I haven't gotten pregnant."

"Do you think one of us might have some kind of problem? Should we see a doctor?"

"No, I don't think so. I think we're both fine, it's just taking awhile."

"Well, if you don't get pregnant within the next year, I insist we try to find out why."

Sandy, still not looking at him, said, "Okay, we'll wait another year."

Len thought to himself, Why would Sandy not want to get checked by a doctor now? Isn't she eager like I am to have children? Something just doesn't make sence.

A few days later, on Saturday, Len was home by himself and Sandy was out grocery shopping. Len usually went shopping with her, but he had a bad cold. He started sneezing again and went to the bedroon to get another hankie out of his drawer. He said, "Oh no! All my hankies are gone! They all must be in the hamper to be washed. I sure do need one now!"

He then thought, I bet Sandy has some in one of her drawers. I'm sure she won't mind if I borrow a few. Len started looking in the top drawer but didn't find any hankies. He then started checking the rest of the drawers. He finally got to the bottom drawer and thought, Well, if the hankies aren't here, Sandy must not have any. He opened the bottom drawer and started searching through it.

As he was searching, he found a bottle of pills. He thought, What in the heck are these? He looked at the lable and they were called Triphasil, then thought, Aren't these the pills that keep a woman from getting pregnant? I know these have to be Sandy's pills because her name is on this bottle and it is a current date. I can't believe this! Why would Sandy be taking these pills? She should be home soon and I'm going to ask her what's going on! I'm really upset! Might we have had a child by now if it wasn't for these birth control pills!

About half an hour later, Sandy pulled into the drive way. She entered the house and yelled, "Len, please help me bring the groceries in."

Len came down the stairs, walked up to her and put both his hands on her shoulders. He looked her straight in the eyes and said, "I'm not bringing any groceries in until you explain to me what these pills were doing in your drawer!"

Sandy looked at him and started crying. She sat down on the couch and cried even harded.

Len sat next to her and said, "I have no idea what is going on here, but you better tell me now!"

Sandy cried and said, "I don't want to talk about it! Long ago, you told me that you didn't care why I left you for a year and never even got in touch with you. You said it didn't matter."

"If it has something to do with you taking these pills, I do want to know, right now!"

Sandy was now hysterical! "I'm not saying anything!"

"You better, or you'll be sorry!"

"Len, I love you so much, I will tell you the story, but you aren't going to like it!" She then heard something in her head say,

"I GOT YOU NOW!"